Antarctica

Antarctica

CLAIRE KEEGAN

Atlantic Monthly Press
New York

Originally published in the United Kingdom by Faber and Faber in 1999.

Published simultaneously in Canada
Printed in the United States of America

FIRST AMERICAN EDITION

Library of Congress Cataloging-in-Publication Data
Keegan, Claire.
    Antartica / Claire Keegan.
      p. cm.
    ISBN 0-87113-779-8
      1. Ireland—Social life and customs—20th century—Fiction.
    2. Southern States—Social life and customs—Fiction.   I. Title.
    PR6061.E329 A82 2001
    823'.914—dc21   00-049604

Atlantic Monthly Press
841 Broadway
New York, NY 10003

01 02 03 04   10 9 8 7 6 5 4 3 2 1

For Padraig Hickey and in memory of John McCarron

Contents

Antarctica

Antarctica

Every time the happily married woman went away, she wondered how it would feel to sleep with another man. That weekend she was determined to find out. It was December; she felt a curtain closing on another year. She wanted to do this before she got too old. She was sure she would be disappointed.

On Friday evening, she took the train into the city, sat reading in a first-class carriage. The book didn't hold her interest; she could already predict the ending. Beyond the window lighted houses flashed past her in the darkness. She had left a dish of macaroni and cheese out for the kids, brought her husband's suits back from the cleaners. She'd told him she was going shopping for Christmas. He'd no reason not to trust her.

When she reached the city, she took a taxi to the hotel. They gave her a small, white room with a view of Vicar's Close, one of the oldest streets in England, a row of stone houses with tall, granite chimneys where the clergy lived. That night she sat at the hotel bar drinking tequila and lime. Old men were reading newspapers, business was slow, but she didn't mind, she needed a good night's sleep. She fell into her rented bed, into a dreamless sleep and woke to the sound of bells ringing in the cathedral.

On Saturday she walked to the shopping center. Families were out, pushing buggies through the morning crowd, a thick stream of people flowing through automatic doors. She bought unusual gifts for her children, things she thought they wouldn't predict. She bought an electric razor for her eldest son, he was getting to that age, an atlas for the girl, and for her husband an expensive gold watch with a plain, white face.

She dressed up in the afternoon, put on a short plum-colored dress, high heels, her darkest lipstick, and walked back into town. A jukebox song, "The Ballad of Lucy Jordan," lured her into a pub, a converted prison with barred windows and a low, beamed ceiling. Fruit machines blinked in one corner, and just as she sat on the bar stool, a little battalion of coins fell into a chute.

"Hello," the fellow next to her said. "Haven't seen you before." He had a red complexion, a gold chain inside an open-necked Hawaiian shirt, mud-colored hair, and his glass was almost empty.

"What's that you're drinking?" she asked.

He turned out to be a real talker, told her his life story, how he worked nights at the old folks' home. How he lived alone, was an orphan, had no relations except a distant cousin he'd never met. There was no ring on his finger.

"I'm the loneliest man in the world," he said. "How about you?"

"I'm married." She said it before she knew what she was saying.

He laughed. "Play pool with me."

"I don't know how."

"Doesn't matter," he said. "I'll teach you. You'll be potting that black before you know it." He put coins into a slot and pulled something, and a little landslide of balls knuckled down into a black hole under the table.

"Stripes and solids," he said, chalking up the cue. "You're one or the other. I'll break."

He taught her to lean down low and sight the ball, to watch the cue ball when she took the shot, but he didn't let her win one game. When she went into the ladies' room, she was drunk. She couldn't find the edge of the toilet paper. She leaned her forehead against the cool of the mirror. She couldn't remember ever being drunk like this. They finished off their drinks and went outside. The air spiked her lungs. Clouds smashed into each other in the sky. She hung her head back to look at them. She wished the world could turn into a fabulous, outrageous red to match her mood.

"Let's walk," he said. "I'll give you the tour."

She fell into step beside him, listened to his leather jacket creaking as he led her down a path where the moat curved around the cathedral. An old man stood outside the Bishop's Palace selling stale bread for the birds. They bought some and stood at the water's edge feeding five cygnets whose feathers were turning white. Brown ducks flew across the water and landed in a nice skim on the moat. When a black Labrador came bounding down the path, a huddle of pigeons rose as one and settled magically in the trees.

"I feel like Francis of Assisi," she laughed.

Rain began to fall; she felt it falling on her face like small electric shocks. They backtracked through the market-place, where stalls were set up in the shelter of tarpaulin. They sold everything: smelly secondhand books and china, big red poinsettias, holly wreaths, brass ornaments, fresh fish with dead eyes lying on a bed of ice.

"Come home with me," he said. "I'll cook for you."

"You'll cook for me?"

"You eat fish?"

"I eat everything," she said, and he seemed amused.

"I know your type," he said. "You're wild. You're one of these wild middle-class women."

He chose a trout that looked like it was still alive. The fishmonger chopped its head off and wrapped it up in foil. He bought a tub of black olives and a slab of feta cheese from the Italian woman with the deli stall at the end. He bought limes and Colombian coffee. Always, as they passed the stalls, he asked her if she wanted any-thing. He was free with his money, kept it crumpled in his pockets like old receipts, didn't smooth the notes out even when he was handing them over. On the way home they stopped at the off-license, bought two bottles of Chianti and a lottery ticket, all of which she insisted on paying for.

"We'll split it if we win," she said. "Go to the Bahamas."

"Don't hold your breath," he said, and watched her walk through the door he'd opened for her. They strolled down cobbled streets, past a barber's where a man was sitting with his head back, being shaved. The streets grew narrow and winding; they were outside the city now.

"You live in suburbia?" she asked.

He did not answer, kept walking. She could smell the fish. When they came to a wrought-iron gate, he told her to "hang a left." They passed under an archway and came out in a dead end. He unlocked a door to a block of flats and followed her upstairs to the top floor.

"Keep going," he said when she stopped on the landings. She giggled and climbed, giggled and climbed again, stopped at the top.

The door needed oil; the hinges creaked when he pushed it back. The walls of his flat were plain and pale, the sills dusty. One stained mug stood on the sink. A white Persian cat jumped off a draylon couch in the living room. It was neglected, like a place where someone used to live; dank smells, no sign of a phone, no photographs, no decorations, no Christmas tree. The rubber plant in the living room crawled across the carpet toward a rectangular pool of streetlight.

A big cast-iron tub stood in the bathroom on blue, steel claws.

"Some bath," she said.

"You want a bath?" he asked. "Try it out. Fill her up and dive in. Go ahead, be my guest."

She filled the tub, kept the water hot as she could stand it. He came in and stripped to the waist and shaved at the handbasin with his back to her. She closed her eyes and listened to him work the lather, tapping the razor against the sink, shaving. It was like they'd done it all before. She thought him the least threatening man she'd ever known. She held her nose and slid underwater, listened to the blood pumping in her head, the rush and cloud in her brain. When she surfaced, he was standing there in the steam, wiping traces of shaving foam off his chin, smiling.

"Having fun?" he asked.

When he lathered a washcloth, she stood up. Water fell off her shoulders and trickled down her legs. He began at her feet and worked upward, washing her in strong, slow circles. She looked good in the yellow shaving light, raised her feet and arms and turned like a child for him. He made her sink back down into the water and rinsed her off, wrapped her in a towel.

"I know what you need," he said. "You need looking after. There isn't a woman on the earth who doesn't need looking after. Stay there." He went out and came back with a comb, began combing the knots from her hair. "Look at you," he said. "You're a real blond. You've blond fuzz, like a peach." His knuckle slid down the back of her neck, followed her spine.

His bed was brass with a white, goose-down duvet and black pillowcases. She undid his belt, slid it from the loops. The buckle jingled when it hit the floor. She loosened his trousers. Naked, he wasn't beautiful, yet there was something voluptuous about him, something unbreakable and sturdy in his build. His skin was hot.

"Pretend you're America," she said. "I'll be Columbus."

Under the bedclothes, down between the damp of his thighs, she explored his nakedness. His body was a novelty. When her feet became entangled in the sheets, he flung them off. She had surprising strength in bed, an urgency that bruised him. She pulled his head back by the hair, drank in the smell of strange soap on his neck. He kissed her and kissed her. There wasn't any hurry. His palms were the rough hands of a working man. They battled against their lust, wrestled against what in the end carried them away.

Afterward they smoked; she hadn't smoked in years, quit before the first baby. She was reaching over for the ashtray when she saw a shotgun cartridge behind his clock radio.

"What's this?" She picked it up. It was heavier than it looked.

"Oh that. That's a present for somebody."

"Some present," she said. "Looks like pool isn't the only thing you shoot."

"Come here."

She snuggled up against him, and they fell swiftly into sleep, the sweet sleep of children, and woke in darkness, hungry.

While he took charge of dinner, she sat on the couch with the cat on her lap and watched a documentary on Antarctica, miles of snow, penguins shuffling against subzero winds, Captain Cook sailing down to find the lost continent. He came out with a tea towel draped across his shoulder and handed her a glass of chilled wine.

[7]

"You," he said, "have a thing for explorers." He leaned down over the back of the couch and kissed her.

"Can I do anything?" she asked.

"No," he said and went back into the kitchen.

She sipped her wine and felt the cold sliding down into her stomach. She could hear him chopping vegetables, the bubble of water boiling on the stove. Dinner smells drifted through the rooms. Coriander, lime juice, onions. She could stay drunk; she could live like this. He came out and laid two places at the table, lit a thick, green candle, folded paper napkins. They looked like small white pyramids under a vigil of flame. She turned the TV off and stroked the cat. Its white hairs fell onto his dark blue dressing gown that was much too big for her. She saw the smoke from another man's fire cross the window, but she did not think about her husband, and her lover never mentioned her home life either, not once.

Instead, over Greek salad and grilled trout, the conversation somehow turned to the subject of hell.

As a child, she had been told that hell was different for everyone, your own worst possible scenario. "I always thought hell would be an unbearably cold place where you stayed half frozen but you never quite lost consciousness and you never really felt anything," she said. "There'd be nothing, only a cold sun and the devil there, watching you." She shivered and shook herself. Her color was high. She put her glass to her lips and tilted her neck back as she swallowed. She had a nice, long neck.

[8]

"In that case," he said, "hell for me would be deserted; there'd be nobody there. Not even the devil. I've always taken heart in the fact that hell is populated; all my friends will be there." He ground more pepper over his salad plate and tore the doughy heart out of the loaf.

"The nun at school told us it would last for all eternity," she said, pulling the skin off her trout. "And when we asked how long eternity lasted, she said: 'Think of all the sand in the world, all the beaches, all the sand quarries, the ocean beds, the deserts. Now imagine all that sand in an hourglass, like a gigantic egg timer. If one grain of sand drops every year, eternity is the length of time it takes for all the sand in the world to pass through that glass.' Just think! That terrified us. We were very young."

"You don't still believe in hell," he said.

"No. Can't you tell? If only Sister Emmanuel could see me now, fucking a complete stranger, what a laugh." She broke off a flake of trout and ate it with her fingers.

He put his cutlery down, folded his hands in his lap, and looked at her. She was full now, playing with her food.

"So you think all your friends will be in hell too," she said. "That's nice."

"Not by your nun's definition."

"You have lots of friends? I suppose you know people from work."

"A few," he said. "And you?"

"I have two good friends," she said. "Two people I'd die for."

[9]

"You're lucky," he said, and got up to make the coffee.

That night, he was ravenous, like a man leasing himself out to her. There was nothing he wouldn't do.

"You're a very generous lover," she said afterward, passing him the cigarette. "You're very generous period."

The cat jumped up on the bed and startled her.

"Jesus Christ!" she said. There was something creepy about his cat.

Cigarette ash fell on the duvet, but they were too drunk to care. Drunk and careless and occupying the same bed on the same night. It was all so simple, really. Loud Christmas music started up in the apartment downstairs. A Gregorian chant, monks singing.

"Who's your neighbor?"

"Oh, some granny. Deaf as a coot. She sings, too. She's on her own down there, keeps odd hours."

They settled down to sleep, she with her head captured in the crook of his shoulder. He stroked her arm, petting her like an animal. She imitated the cat purring, rolling her r's the way they'd taught her in Spanish class, while hailstones rapped the windowpanes.

"I'll miss you when you go."

She said nothing, just lay there watching the red numbers on his clock radio change until she drifted off.

On Sunday she woke early. A white frost had fallen in the night. She dressed, watched him sleeping, his head on the black pillow. In the bathroom she looked inside the cabinet. It was empty. In the living room, she read the titles of his books. They were arranged in alphabetical order.

She walked back along treacherous pavements to check out of her hotel. She got lost and had to ask a troubled-looking lady with a poodle where to go. A huge Christmas tree sparkled in the lobby. Her suitcase lay open on the bed. Her clothes smelled of cigarette smoke. She showered and changed. The cleaning lady knocked at ten, but she waved her off, told her not to bother, told her nobody should work on Sundays.

In the lobby, she sat in the telephone booth and called home. She asked about the children, the weather, asked her husband about his day, told him about the children's gifts. She would return to untidy, cluttered rooms, dirty floors, cut knees, a hall with mountain bikes and roller skates. Questions. She hung up, became aware of a presence behind her, waiting.

"You never said good-bye." She felt breath on her neck.

He was standing there, a black wool cap pulled down low over his ears, hiding his forehead.

"You were sleeping," she said.

"You sneaked off," he said. "You're a sneaky one."

"I —"

"You want to sneak off to lunch and get drunk?" He pushed her into the booth and kissed her, a long, wet kiss. "I woke this morning with your scent in the sheets," he said. "It was beautiful."

"Bottle it," she said, "we'll make a fortune."

They ate lunch in a place with six-foot walls, arched windows, and a flagstone floor. Their table was next to the fire. Over plates of roast beef and Yorkshire pudding they got drunk again, but they didn't talk much. She drank Bloody Marys, told the waitress to go heavy on the Tabasco. He started on ale then switched to gin and tonics, anything to stave off the imminent prospect of their separation.

"I don't normally drink like this," she said. "How about you?"

"Nah," he said, and signaled the waitress for another round.

They dawdled over dessert and the Sunday newspapers. The landlady came around and threw more wood on the fire. Once, while turning a page of the newspaper, she looked up. He was staring intently at her mouth.

"Smile," he said.

"What?"

"Smile."

She smiled, and he reached over and pressed the tip of his index finger against her tooth.

"There," he said, showing her a tiny speck of food. "It's gone now."

When they walked out onto the marketplace, a thick fog had fallen on the town, so thick she could hardly read the signs. A straggle of Sunday vendors, out to win the Christmas trade, were demonstrating their wares.

"Done your Christmas shopping?" she asked.

"Nah, got nobody to buy for, have I? I'm an orphan. Remember?"

"I'm sorry."

"Come on. Let's walk."

He gripped her hand and took her down a dirt road that led into a black wood beyond the houses. He held her tight; her fingers hurt.

"You're hurting me," she said.

He loosened his hold, but he did not say sorry. Light drained out of the day. Dusk stoked the sky, bribing daylight into darkness. They walked for a long time without talking, just feeling the Sunday hush, listening to the trees straining against the icy wind.

"I was married once, went off to Africa for a honeymoon," he said suddenly. "It didn't last. I had a big house, furniture, all that. She was a good woman, too, a wonderful gardener. You know that plant in my living room? Well, that was hers. I've been waiting for years for that plant to die, but the fucking thing, it keeps on growing."

She pictured the plant sprawled across the floor, the length of a grown man, its pot no bigger than a small saucepan, dried roots snarling up over the pot. A miracle it was still alive.

"Some things you just have no control over," he said, scratching his head. "She said I wouldn't last a year without her. Boy, was she wrong." He looked at her then, and smiled, a strange smile of victory.

They had walked deep into the woods by now; except for the sound of their footsteps on the road and the ribbon of sky between the trees, she could not have been sure where the path was. He grabbed her suddenly and pulled her in under the trees, pushed her back against a tree trunk. She couldn't see. She felt the bark through her coat, his belly against hers, could smell gin on his breath.

"You won't forget me," he said, smoothing her hair back from her eyes. "Say it. Say you won't forget me."

"I won't forget you."

In the darkness, he ran his fingers across her face, as if he was a blind man trying to memorize her. "Nor I, you. A little piece of you will be ticking right here," he said, taking her hand and placing it inside his shirt. She felt his heart beneath his hot skin, beating. He kissed her then as if there was something in her mouth he wanted. Words, probably. At that moment the cathedral bells rang, and she wondered what time it was. Her train left at six, but she was all packed, there was no real hurry.

"Did you check out this morning?"

"Yes," she laughed. "They think I'm the tidiest guest they've ever had. My bag's in the lobby."

"Come to my place. I'll get you a taxi, see you off."

She wasn't in the mood for sex. In her mind she was already gone, was facing her husband in the station. She felt clean and full and warm; all she wanted now was a good snooze on the train. But in the end she could think of no reason not to go and, yielding like a parting gift to him, said yes.

They retreated from the darkness of the woods, walked down Vicar's Close, and emerged below the moat near the hotel. The seagulls were inland. They hovered above the waterfowl, swooping down and snapping up the bread a bunch of Americans were throwing to the swans. She collected her suitcase and walked the slippery streets to his place. The rooms were cold. Yesterday's dirty dishes lay soaking in the sink, a rim of greasy water on the steel. Remnant daylight filtered through gaps between the curtains, but he did not turn a light on.

"Come here," he said. He took his jacket off and knelt before her. He unlaced her boots, undid the knots slowly, peeled her stockings off, eased her underwear down around her ankles. He stood up and took her coat off, opened her blouse carefully, admired the buttons, unzipped her skirt, slid her watch down over her hand. Then he reached up under her hair and took her earrings out. They were dangly earrings, gold leaves her husband had given her for their anniversary. He stripped her; he had all the time in the world. She felt like a child being put to bed. She didn't have to do anything with him, for him. No duties, all she had to do was be there.

"Lie back," he said.

Naked, she fell back into the goose down.

"I could go to sleep," she said, shutting her eyes.

"Not yet," he said.

The room was cold, but he was sweating; she could smell his sweat. He pinned her wrists above her head with one hand and kissed her throat. A drop of sweat fell onto her neck. A drawer opened and something jingled. Handcuffs. She was startled but did not think fast enough to object.

"You'll like this," he said. "Trust me."

He bound her wrists to the head of the brass bedstead. A section of her mind panicked. There was something de-

[15]

Claire Keegan

liberate about him, something silent and overpowering. More sweat fell on her. She tasted the tangy salt on his skin. He retreated and advanced, made her ask for it, made her come.

He got up. He went out and left her there, handcuffed to the headboard. The kitchen light came on. She smelled coffee, heard him breaking eggs. He came in with a tray and sat over her.

"I have to—"

"Don't move." He spoke quietly. He was dead calm.

"Take these off—"

"Shhhhh," he said. "Eat. Eat before you go." He extended a bite of scrambled egg on a fork, and she swallowed it. It tasted of salt and pepper. She turned her head. The clock read 5:32.

"Christ, look at the time—"

"Don't swear," he said. "Eat. And drink. Drink this. I'll get the keys."

"Why won't you—"

"Just take a drink. Come on. I drank with you, remember?"

Still handcuffed, she drank the coffee he tilted from the mug. It took only a minute. A warm, dark feeling spread over her, and then she slept.

When she woke, he was standing in the harsh fluorescent light, dressing. She was still handcuffed to the bed. She tried to speak, but she was gagged. One of her ankles, too, was bound to the foot of the bed with another pair of handcuffs. He continued dressing, snapping his denim shirt closed.

"I have to go to work," he said, tying his bootlaces. "It can't be helped."

He went out, came back in with a basin. "In case you need it," he said, leaving it on the bed. He tucked her in and kissed her then, a quick, normal kiss, and turned the light out. He stopped in the hall and turned to face her. His shadow loomed over the bed. Her eyes were very big and pleading. She was reaching out to him with her eyes. He held his hands out, showing his palms.

"It's not what you think," he said. "It really isn't. I love you, you see. Try to understand."

And then he turned and left. She listened to him leave, heard him on the stairs, a zipper closing. The hall light was doused, the door banged, she heard his walk on the pavement, footsteps ebbing.

Frantic, she did her best to undo the handcuffs. She did everything to get free. She was a strong woman. She tried to disconnect the headboard, but when she nudged the sheet back, she could see that it was bolted to the frame. For a long time she rattled the bed. She wanted to yell, "Fire!" That's what police told women to yell in emergencies, but she couldn't chew through the cloth. She managed to get her loose foot on the floor and thumped the carpet. Then she remembered granny, deaf, downstairs. Hours passed before she calmed down to think and listen. Her breathing steadied. She heard the curtain flapping in the next room. He'd left the window open. The duvet had fallen on the floor in all the fuss, and she was naked. She couldn't reach it. Cold was moving in, spilling into the house, filling up the rooms. She shivered. Cold air falls, she thought. Eventually, the shivering stopped. Chronic numbness spread through her; she imagined the blood slowing in her veins, her heart shrinking. The cat sprang up and landed on the bed, prowled the mattress. Her dulled rage changed to terror. That too passed. The curtain in the next room slapped the wall faster now: the wind was rising. She thought of him and felt nothing. She thought about her husband and her children. They might never find her. She might never see them again. It didn't matter. She could see her own breath in the gloom, feel the cold closing over her head. It began to dawn on her, a cold, slow sun bleaching the east. Was it her imagination or was that snow falling beyond the windowpanes? She watched the clock on his bedside table, the red numbers changing. The cat was watching her, his eyes dark as apple seeds. She thought of Antarctica, the snow and ice and the bodies of dead explorers. Then she thought of hell, and then eternity.

Men and Women

My father takes me places. He has artificial hips so he needs me to open gates. To reach our house you must drive up a long lane through a wood, open two sets of gates and close them behind you so the sheep won't escape to the road. I'm handy. I open the gates, my father freewheels the Volkswagen through, I close the gates behind him and hop back into the passenger seat. To save petrol, he starts the car on the run, gathering speed on the slope before the road, and then we're off to wherever my father is going on that particular day.

Sometimes it's the scrap yard, where he's looking for a spare part, or, scenting a bargain in some classified ad, we wind up in a farmer's mucky field, pulling cabbage plants or picking seed potatoes in a dusty shed. At the forge I stare into the water barrel, whose surface reflects patches of the milky skies that drift past, sluggish, until the blacksmith plunges the red hot metal down and scorches away the clouds. On Saturdays, my father goes to the mart and examines sheep in the pens, feeling their backbones, looking into their mouths. If he buys just a few sheep, he doesn't bother going home for the trailer but puts them in the back of the car, and it is my job to sit between the front seats and keep them there. They shit small pebbles and say baaaah!, the Suffolks' tongues dark as the raw liver we cook on Mondays. I keep them back until we get to whichever house Da stops at for a feed on the way home. Usually it's Bridie Knox's because Bridie kills her own stock and there's always meat. The hand brake doesn't work, so when Da parks in her yard, I get out and put the stone behind the wheel.

I am the girl of a thousand uses.

"Be the holy, Missus, what way are ya?"

"Dan!" Bridie says, like she didn't hear the car.

Bridie lives in a smoky little house without a husband, but she has sons who drive tractors around the fields. They're small, deeply unattractive men who smell of dung and patch their Wellingtons. Bridie wears red lipstick and face powder, but her hands are like a man's hands. I think her head is wrong for her body, the way my dolls look when I swap their heads.

"Have you aer a bit for the child, Missus? She's hungry at home," Da says, looking at me like I'm one of those African children we give up sugar for during Lent.

"Ah now!" says Bridie, smiling at his old joke. "That girl looks fed to me. Sit down there and I'll put the kettle on."

"To tell you the truth, Missus, I wouldn't fall out with a drop of something. I'm after being in at the mart, and the price of sheep is a holy scandal."

He talks about sheep and cattle and the weather and how this little country of ours is in a woeful state while Bridie sets the table, puts out the Chef sauce and the Colman's mustard, and cuts big, thick slices off a flitch of beef or boiled ham. I sit by the window and keep an eye on the sheep, who stare, bewildered, from the car. Da eats everything in front of him while I build a tower of cookies and lick the chocolate off and give the rest to the Jack Russell terrier under the table.

When we get home, I find the fire shovel and collect the sheep droppings from the car and roll barley on the loft.

"Where did you go?" Mammy asks.

I tell her all about our travels while we carry buckets of calf nuts and beet pulp across the yard. Da sits in under the shorthorn cow and milks her into a zinc bucket.

My brother sits in the sitting room beside the fire and pretends he's studying. He will do the Inter-cert. Next year. My brother is going to be somebody, so he doesn't open gates or clean up shit or carry buckets. All he does is read and write and draw triangles with special pencils Da buys him for mechanical drawing. He is the brains in the family. He stays there until he is called to dinner.

"Go down and tell Seamus his dinner is on the table," Da says.

I have to take off my Wellingtons before I go down.

"Come up and get it, you lazy fucker," I say.

"I'll tell," he says.

"You won't," I say, and go back up to the kitchen, where I spoon garden peas onto his plate because he won't eat turnip or cabbage like the rest of us.

Evenings, I get my school bag and do homework on the kitchen table while Ma watches the television we rent for winter. On Tuesdays she makes a big pot of tea before eight o'clock and sits at the range and glues herself to the program where a man teaches a woman how to drive a car. How to change gears, to let the clutch out and give her the juice. Except for a rough woman up behind the hill who drives a tractor and a Protestant woman in the town, no woman we know drives. During the break, her eyes leave the screen and travel to the top shelf of the dresser, where she has hidden the spare key to the Volkswagen in the old cracked teapot. I am not supposed to know this. I sigh and continue tracing the course of the River Shannon through a piece of waxed paper.

On Christmas Eve, I put up signs. I cut up a cardboard box, and in red marker, I write, "THIS WAY SANTA" and draw arrows, pointing the way. I am always afraid he will get lost or not bother coming because the gates are too much trouble. I staple them onto the paling at the end of the lane and on the timber gates and one inside the door leading down to the parlor, where the tree is. I put a glass of stout and a piece of cake on the hearth and conclude that Santa must be drunk as a lord by Christmas morning.

Daddy takes his good hat out of the press and looks at himself in the mirror. It's a fancy hat with a stiff feather stuck down in the brim. He tightens it well down on his head to hide his bald patch.

"And where are you going on Christmas Eve?" Mammy asks.

"Going off to see a man about a pup," he says, and bangs the door.

I go to bed and have trouble sleeping. I am the only person in my class Santa Claus still visits. I know this because the master asked, "Who does Santa Claus still come to?" and mine was the only hand raised. I'm different, but every year I feel there is a greater chance that he will not come, that I will become like the others.

I wake at dawn, and Mammy is already lighting the fire, kneeling on the hearth, ripping up newspaper, smiling. There is a terrible moment when I think maybe Santa didn't come because I said, "Come and get it, you lazy fucker," but he does come. He leaves me the Tiny Tears doll I asked for, wrapped in the same wrapping paper we have, and I think how the postal system is like magic, how I can send a letter two days before Christmas, and it reaches the North Pole overnight, even though it takes a week for a letter to reach England. Santa does not come to Seamus anymore. I suspect he knows what Seamus is really doing all those evenings in the sitting room, reading *Hit n Run* magazines and drinking the red lemonade out of the sideboard, not using his brains at all.

Nobody's up except Mammy and me. We are the early birds. We make tea, eat toast and chocolate fingers for breakfast. Then she puts on her best apron, the one dappled with strawberries, and turns on the radio, chops onions and parsley while I grate a plain loaf into crumbs. We stuff the turkey and waltz around the kitchen. Seamus and Da come down and investigate the parcels under the tree. Seamus gets a dartboard for Christmas. He hangs it on the back door, and himself and Da throw darts and chalk up scores

Claire Keegan

while Mammy and me put on our anoraks and feed the pigs
and cattle and sheep and let the hens out.

"How come they do nothing?" I ask. I am reaching
into warm straw, feeling for eggs. The hens lay less in
winter.

"They're men," she says, as if this explains everything.

Because it is Christmas, I say nothing. I come inside, and
duck when a dart flies past my head.

"Ha! Ha!" says Seamus.

"Bull's-eye," says Da.

On New Year's Eve, it snows. Snowflakes land and melt
on the window ledges. It is the end of another year. I eat
a bowl of sherry trifle for breakfast and fall asleep watching *Lassie* on TV. I play with my dolls after dinner but get
fed up filling Tiny Tears with water and squeezing it out
through the hole in her backside, so I take her head off,
but her neck is too thick to fit into my other dolls' bodies.
I start playing darts with Seamus. He chalks two marks
on the linoleum, one for him and another, closer to the
board, for me. When I get a triple nineteen, Seamus says,
"Fluke." According to my brother, anything I do right is
an accident.

"Eighty-seven," I say, toting up my score. I'm quick to
add even though I'm no good at subtraction.

"Fluke!" he says.

"You don't know what fluke is," I say. "Fluke and
worms. Look it up in the dictionary."

"Exactly," he says.

I am fed up being treated like a child. I wish I was big. I wish I could sit beside the fire and be called up to dinner and draw triangles, lick the nibs of special pencils, sit behind the wheel of a car and have someone open gates that I could drive through. Vrum! Vrum! I'd give her the holly, make a bumper sticker that would read CAUTION, SHEEP ON BOARD.

That night, we get dressed up. Mammy wears a dark red dress, the color of the shorthorn cow. Her skin is freckled like somebody dipped a toothbrush in paint and splattered her. She asks me to fasten the catch on her string of pearls. I used to stand on the bed doing this, but now I'm tall, the tallest girl in my class; the master measured us. Mammy is tall and thin, but the skin on her hands is hard. I wonder if someday she will look like Bridie Knox, become part man, part woman.

Da does not do himself up. I have never known him to take a bath or wash his hair; he just changes his hat and shoes. Now he clamps his good hat down on his head and looks at himself in the mirror. The feather is sticking up more than usual. Then he puts his shoes on. They are big black shoes he bought when he sold the Suffolk ram. He has trouble with the laces, as he finds it hard to stoop. Seamus wears a green sweater with elbow patches, black trousers with legs like tubes, and cowboy boots to make him taller.

"Don't trip up in your high heels," I say.

We get into the Volkswagen, me and Seamus in the back and Mammy and Da up front. Even though I washed the car out, I can smell sheep shit, a faint, pungent odor that always drags us back to where we come from. Da turns on the windscreen wiper; there's only one, and it screeches as it wipes the snow away. Crows rise from the trees, releasing shrill, hungry sounds. Because there are no doors in the back, it is Mammy who gets out to open the gates. I think she is beautiful with her pearls around her throat and her red skirt flaring out when she swings around. I wish my father would get out, that the snow would be falling on him, not on my mother in her good clothes. I've seen other fathers holding their wives' coats, holding doors open, asking if they'd like anything at the shop, bringing home bars of chocolate and ripe pears even when they say no.

Spellman Hall stands in the middle of a car park, an arch of bare, multicolored bulbs surrounding a crooked Merry Christmas sign above the door. Inside is big as a warehouse with a slippy wooden floor and benches at the walls. Strange lights make every white garment dazzle. It's amazing. I can see the newsagent's bra through her blouse, fluff like snow on the auctioneer's trousers. The accountant has a black eye and a sweater made of gray and white wool diamonds. Overhead, a globe of shattered mirror shimmers and spins slowly. At the top of the ball-room a Formica table is stacked with bottles of lemonade and orange, custard cream cookies, and cheese and onion Tayto. The butcher's wife stands behind, handing out the straws and taking in the money. Several of the women I know from my trips around the country are there: Bridie with her haw red lipstick; Sarah Combs, who only last week urged my father to have a glass of sherry and gave me stale cake while she took him into the sitting room to show him her new suite of furniture. Miss Emma Jenkins, who always makes a fry and drinks coffee instead of tea and never has a sweet thing in the house because of something she calls her gastric juices.

On the stage, men in red blazers and candy-striped bow ties play drums, guitars, blow horns, and the Nerves Moran is out front, singing "My Lovely Leitrim." Mammy and I are first out on the floor for the cuckoo waltz, and when the music stops, she dances with Seamus. My father dances with the women from the roads. I wonder how he can dance like that and not open gates. Seamus jives with teenage girls he knows from the vocational school, hand up, arse out, and the girls spinning like blazes. Old men in their thirties ask me out.

"Will ya chance a quickstep?" they ask. Or "How's about a half set?"

They tell me I'm light on my feet.

"Christ, you're like a feather," they say and put me through my paces.

In the Paul Jones, the music stops and I get stuck with a farmer who smells sour like the whiskey we make sick lambs drink in springtime, but the young fella who hushes the cattle around the ring in the mart butts in and rescues me.

"Don't mind him," he says. "He thinks he's the bees knees."

I imagine bees having knees and think it queer. He smells of ropes, new galvanize, Jeyes Fluid, or maybe I'm just imagining it. People say I imagine things.

After the half set I get thirsty, and Mammy gives me a fifty-pence piece for lemonade and raffle tickets. A slow waltz begins, and Da walks across to Sarah Combs, who rises from the bench and takes her jacket off. Her shoulders are bare; I can see the tops of her breasts like two duck eggs. Mammy is sitting with her handbag on her lap, watching. There is something sad about Mammy tonight; it is all around her like when a cow dies and the lorry comes to take it away. Something I don't fully understand is happening, as if a black cloud has drifted in and could burst and cause havoc. I go over and offer her my lemonade, but she just takes a little, dainty sip and thanks me. I give her half my raffle tickets, but she doesn't care. My father has his arms around Sarah Combs, dancing slow like slowness is what he wants. Seamus is leaning against the far wall with his hands in his pockets, smiling down at the blond who hogs the mirror in the ladies'.

"Cut in on Da."

"What?" he says.

"Cut in on Da."

"What would I do that for?" he asks.

"And you're supposed to be the one with all the brains," I say. "Gobshite."

I walk across the floor and tap Sarah Combs on the back. I tap a rib. She turns, her wide, patent belt gleaming in the light spilling from the globe above our heads.

"Excuse me," I say, like I'm going to ask her the time.

"Tee-hee," she says, looking down at me. Her eyeballs are cracked like the teapot on our dresser.

"I want to dance with Daddy."

At the word "daddy," her face changes and she loosens her grip on my father. I take over. The man on the stage is blowing his trumpet now. My father holds my hand tight, like he wants to hurt me. I can see my mother on the bench, reaching into her bag for a hanky. Then she goes to the ladies'. There's a feeling like hatred all around Da. I get the feeling he's helpless, but I don't care. For the first time in my life, I have some power. I can butt in and take over, rescue and be rescued.

There's a general hullabaloo towards midnight. Everybody's out on the floor, knees buckling, handbags swinging. The Nerves Moran counts down the seconds to the new year, and then there's kissing and hugging. Strange men squeeze me, kiss me like they're thirsty and I'm water.

My parents do not kiss. In all my life, back as far as I remember, I have never seen them touch. Once I took a friend upstairs to show her the house.

"This is Mammy's room," I said, "and this is Daddy's room."

"Your parents don't sleep in the same room?" she said in a voice of pure amazement.

The band picks up the pace. "Oh hokey, hokey, pokey!"

"Work off them turkey dinners, shake off them plum

puddings!" shouts the Nerves Moran, and even the ball-
room show-offs give up on their figures of eight and do
the twist and jive around and I knock my backside against
the mart fella's backside and wind up swinging with a
stranger.

Everybody stands for the national anthem. Da is wiping his forehead with a handkerchief, and Seamus is
panting because he's not used to exercise. The lights
come up, and nothing is the same. People are red-faced
and sweaty; everything's back to normal. The auctioneer takes over the microphone and thanks a whole lot of
different people, and then they auction off a Charolais
calf and a goat and batches of tea and sugar and buns
and jam, plum puddings, and mince pies. There's shit
where the goat stood, and I wonder who'll clean it up.
Not until the very last does the raffle take place. The
auctioneer holds out the cardboard box of stubs to the
blond.

"Dig deep," he says. "No peeping. First prize a bottle
of whiskey."

She takes her time, lapping up the attention.

"Come on," he says. "Good girl, it's not the sweep-
stakes."

She hands him the ticket.

It's a, what color would ya say that is, Jimmy? It's a, a
salmon-colored ticket, number seven hundred and twenty-
five. Seven two five. Serial number 3X429H. I'll give ye that
again."

Men and Women

It's not mine, but I'm close. I don't want the whiskey anyhow; it'd be kept for the pet lambs. I'd rather the box of Afternoon Tea cookies that's coming up next. There's a general shuffle, a search in handbags, arse pockets. The auctioneer calls out the numbers again, and it looks like he'll have to draw another ticket, when Mammy rises from her seat. Head held high, she walks in a straight line across the floor. A space opens in the crowd, people step aside to let her pass. Her new, high-heeled shoes say clipety-clipety on the slippy floor, and her red skirt is flaring. I have never seen her do this. Usually, she's too shy, gives me the tickets, and I run up and collect the prize.

"Do ya like a drop of the booze, do ya Missus?" the Nerves Moran asks, reading her ticket. "Sure wouldn't it keep ya warm on a night like tonight? No woman needs a man if she has a drop of Powers. Isn't that right? Seven twenty-five, that's the one."

My mother is standing there in her elegant clothes, and it's all wrong. She doesn't belong up there.

"Let's check the serial numbers now," he says, drawing it out. "I'm sorry, Missus, wrong serial number. The hubby may keep you warm again tonight. Back to the old reliable."

My mother turns and walks clipety-clipety back down the slippy floor, with everybody knowing she thought she'd won when she didn't win. And suddenly she is no longer walking, but running, running down in the bright white light, past the cloakroom, towards the door, her hair flailing out like a horse's tail behind her.

[31]

* * *

Out in the car park, snow has accumulated on the frozen grass, the evergreen shelter beds, but the tarmac is wet and shiny in the headlights of cars leaving. Thick, unwavering moonlight shines steadily down on the earth. Ma, Seamus, and me sit in the car, shivering, waiting for Da. We can't turn on the engine to heat the car because Da has the keys. My feet are cold as stones. A cloud of greasy steam rises from the open hatch of the chip van, a fat brown sausage painted on the chrome. All around us people are leaving, waving, calling out "Goodnight!'" and "Happy new year!" They're collecting their chips and driving off.

The chip van has closed its hatch and the car park is empty when Da comes out. He gets into the driver's seat, the ignition catches, a splutter, and then we're off, climbing the hill outside the village, winding around the narrow roads towards home.

"That wasn't a bad band," Da says.

Mammy says nothing.

"I said, there was a bit of life in that band." Louder this time.

Still Mammy says nothing.

My father begins to sing. He always sings when he's angry, pretends he's in a good humor when he's raging. The lights of the town are behind us now. These roads are dark. We pass houses with lighted candles in the windows, bulbs blinking on Christmas trees, sheets of newspaper held down on the windscreens of parked cars. Da stops singing before the end of the song.

"Did you see aer a nice little thing in the hall, Seamus?"

"Nothing I'd be mad about."

"That blond was a nice bit of stuff."

I think about the mart, all the men at the rails bidding for heifers and ewes. I think about Sarah Combs and how she always smells of grassy perfume when we go to her house.

The chestnut tree's boughs at the end of our lane are caked with snow. Da stops the car, and we roll back a bit until he puts his foot on the brake. He is waiting for Mammy to get out and open the gates.

Mammy doesn't move.

"Have you got a pain?" he asks her.

She looks straight ahead.

"Is that door stuck or what?" he asks.

"Open it yourself."

He reaches across her and opens her door, but she slams it shut.

"Get out there and open that gate!" he barks at me.

Something tells me I should not move.

"Seamus!" he shouts. "Seamus!"

There's not a budge out of any of us.

"By Jeeesus!" he says.

I am afraid. Outside, one corner of my THIS WAY SANTA sign has come loose, the soggy cardboard flapping in the wind. Da turns to my mother, his voice filled with venom.

"And you walking up in your finery in front of all the neighbors, thinking you'd won first prize in the raffle."

[33]

He laughs and opens his door. "Running like a tinker out of the hall."

He gets out and there's rage in his walk, as if he's walking on hot coals. He sings: "Far Away in Australia!" He is reaching up, taking the wire off the gate when a gust of wind blows his hat off. The gates swing open. He stoops to retrieve his hat, but the wind nudges it farther from his reach. He takes another few steps and stoops again to retrieve it, but again it is blown just out of his reach. I think of Santa Claus using the same wrapping paper as us, and suddenly I understand. There is only one, obvious explanation.

My father is getting smaller. It feels as though the trees are moving, the chestnut tree whose green hands shelter us in summer is backing away. Then I realize it's the car. It's us. We are rolling, sliding backwards without a hand brake and I am not out there putting the stone behind the wheel. And that is when Mammy takes the steering. She slides over into my father's seat and puts her foot on the brake. We stop going backwards. She revs up the engine and puts the car in gear, the gearbox grinds, she hasn't the clutch in far enough, but then there's a splutter and we're moving. Mammy is taking us forward, past the Santa sign, past my father, who has stopped singing, through the open gates. She drives us through the fresh snow. I can smell the pines. When I look back, my father is standing there watching our taillights. The snow is falling on him, on his bare head while he stands there, clutching his hat.

Where the Water's Deepest

The au pair sits on the edge of the pier this night, fishing. Beside her, cheese she salvaged from the salad bowl at dinner, her leather sandals. She removes the band from her ponytail and shakes her hair loose. Leftover smells of cooking and bathsuds drift down from the house through the trees. She slides a cube of cheese onto the hook and casts. Her wrist is good. The line makes a perfect arc in the air, drops down and vanishes. Slowly she reels it toward her, where the water's deepest. She's caught a nice perch this way before.

Lately she's not been sleeping well, wakes to the same dream. She and the boy are in the yard at evening time. Wind bloats the clothes on the line and black trees are nuzzling overhead. Then the ground trembles. Stars drop and jingle around their feet like coins. The barn roof shudders, lifts off like a great metal leaf, scraping clouds. The earth fractures open, and the boy is left standing on the other side.

"Jump! Jump, I'll catch you!" she yells.

The boy is smiling. He trusts her.

"Come on!" she holds her arms open wide. "Jump! It's so easy!"

He runs fast and jumps. His feet clear the canyon, but then the strangest thing happens: her hands melt and the

Claire Keegan

boy drops backwards into the darkness. The au pair just stands on the edge and watches him fall.

Sometimes she dreams this twice in the same night. Last night she got up and smoked a cigarette in the bathroom and watched the moon. The light slid off the gold-plated taps, dipped into the porcelain sink, making shadow. She brushed her teeth and went back to bed.

That afternoon they'd dug up worms and carried their fishing gear down to the lakeshore. The au pair flipped the boat right side up and slid it onto the water, held it steady for the boy. "Right-ho!" she said and rowed them out past the shade of the pier. The boy was wearing a Red Sox baseball cap his father had brought back from a business trip. Freckles had grown together across his nose; the scab on his knee was healing. His hand dangled over the side and tore the water's surface as she rowed. When she raised the oars, they drifted into a black cloud of mosquitoes.

"Do they have bugs in the reef?" the boy asked.

The au pair's voice changed when she talked about home. She talked as if she could reach out through the past and touch it with her hands. She baited his hook, told him how she'd learned to scuba dive and snorkel with a spear, explored the hidden world under the ocean. Gigantic mountains where the fish swam in schools and changed direction all at once. Seaweed swirling. A turtle with great spirals on his back, swimming past. Seahorses.

"I wanna go scuba diving here," the boy said.

[36]

"We can't, love. Your lake's too dark and muddy; the bottom isn't sandy like the ocean—it's mud. Mud deeper than two grown men standing one on top of the other. Way too dangerous for diving."

The boy turned quiet for a while. Quarter horses in the far meadow whinnied and cantered down the hill, snorted to a stop at the water's edge.

"Let's play What's It Like!" she said and slapped a bug on her arm.

The boy shrugged. "Okay."

She took the first turn: "This boat is like one half of a big brazil nut."

"Your head is like a cabbage."

"Your eyelashes are the color of a palomino's mane."

"What's that?" the boy asked.

"A horse. I'll show you a picture sometime."

"I've eyes like a horse?"

"Your turn."

"Your farts are like baked beans."

"Your farts are like deadly silences," she said.

"You're like a mama," he said, and looked into her eyes.

"Speaking of mamas," she said, "your mama should be home soon. We better get on home." She gripped the oars and rowed them back to shore.

Easter is coming. Before dinner they sat on rugs in the den and made cards out of thick, expensive paper his mama bought downtown and called each other partner: "Merry Easter, Partner. Eat lotsa eggs," his card read. She held his hand, wrote the letters for him, but he told her what to write. He drew the Xs on the bottom by himself. On the front, in crayon, he drew two stick figures on a brown background.

"What are those?" his father asked. A big, red-haired man with Irish ancestors and eyes an unrelenting shade of blue. He was smoking a cigar, watching CNN with his feet up.

"Scuba divers," the boy said.

"I see," he said. "Come here, son."

The boy rose and climbed up on his father's lap.

"Take a break, sweetheart," the man told the au pair.

She got up. She passed the dishes in the kitchen sink, walked out into the night, and slammed the door.

Down at the lake the au pair hears the toilet flush, then the swash of bathwater in the pipes. Bedtime. The boy's mama, a tall, blond woman with high cheekbones who runs a real estate agency downtown, always puts the boy to bed. That is the arrangement. She bathes the boy, reads *Green Eggs and Ham* or *Where the Wild Things Are*. His mama is well educated. Sometimes she reads from a book of poems by Robert Frost and plays Mozart on the stereo. Later, the au pair will go in and see if the boy is still awake, she will turn the night-light on in the bathroom and kiss him good night.

Last winter they traveled north, a three-hour flight to New York City for a long weekend. They stayed in a hotel suite nineteen floors up with a small balcony and a view of Manhattan. That evening the boy's mama dressed up in a loose silk dress and a mink jacket, took her husband's arm, and they went out to dinner. The au pair ordered pizza fungi and Coca-Colas from room service, played Snakes and Ladders with the boy. He threw the dice, and they climbed and slithered up and down the board till bedtime. The au pair stayed up, took a hot shower, and wrapped herself in the fluffy dressing gown with the Hilton crest impressed on the lapel. She opened the balcony door and from the armchair watched the skyline, the evening bleeding into darkness behind the tallest buildings, but she didn't dare go out and look down. Instead, she wrote letters home, saying she might not be back for Christmas after all, how she missed the ocean but they were good to her, she wanted for nothing.

It was late when they got back. She'd dozed off in the chair, but woke to hear them talking in the bedroom. Then the talking stopped, and the man went out on the balcony. Cigar smoke and freezing cold air drifted back into the room. He came back in and bolted the balcony doors and sat on the edge of the couch looking down at her. He smelled of vodka and Polo aftershave, and the au pair felt the cold off his good wool suit.

"You know what happens if we lose the baby, don't you?" he said. "We lose the baby, we lose a baby-sitter. You keep those balcony doors locked, sweetheart, or you'll be taking the first plane home." He kissed her then, a strange, deliberate kiss, an airport kiss for someone you're

[39]

glad to see the back of, then got up and went back in to his wife.

When she heard his snores, she rose and stepped out on the balcony. A weak wind was driving large snow-flakes across the air, sifting them into flurries. It was a December night speckled with snow and the hooting of traffic. Soon it would be Christmas. She gripped the rail-ings and looked down. A snarl of angry, yellow taxis clot-ted the intersections on the streets below. She sucked her breath in. She remembered reading somewhere that a fear of heights masks an attraction to falling. Suddenly, that made some kind of terrifying sense to her. If she didn't think of jumping off, standing on the edge wouldn't cost her a thought. She imagined falling, imagined how that might feel, to dive down, be lost like that, mean everything for moments only, then be gone. She imagined the relief of having everything over and done with; then she backed inside and locked the doors.

The next morning they planned to visit F.A.O. Schwarz. In the lobby, the au pair wrote the boy's name and his room number on a slip of paper and pinned it to the in-side of his trouser pocket.

"Now give this to the nearest policeman if you get lost."

"But I won't get lost!" he said.

"Of course you won't."

It is dark now down at the lake. The au pair senses move-ment in the bushes at the far bank. Somewhere in those fields are wild boars. Once the boy's father trapped a boar, paid a man to slaughter the animal, and stacked the deep-freeze solid. Another dozen casts or so, and she'll turn in. The cheese is nearly used up anyhow. She listens to the frogs ribbuting and for some reason remembers the tock tock of the electric fence back home. Her father taught her never to touch it with the palm, always the back of the hand; that way the reflex would make her pull away, not grip it, if the current was still running. Small things, that's what fathers are for, far as she can see. Practicalities. How to tie your shoelaces and buckle your seat belt. She reels in the line and checks the bait, casts again. The bait plops but she can no longer detect the line against the sky.

Nobody sees the boy leave the house. He sneaks down the back steps but doesn't hold on to the railing like he's told. It doesn't matter that his eyes have not adjusted to the darkness; he knows the grassy slope that leads down to the lake. He can see her pale blouse, the sleeve coming up, the elbow whipping back, casting. The boy runs, although he is told never to run near water. Small grunts, like the noises his cousin's doll makes when he turns her upside down and right side up again, come from his chest. The au pair has her back to him. The boy's feet are soundless; he is silent as a panther in the cool grass.

The au pair doesn't turn her head until his foot hits the first plank of the pier.

"Yoo-hoo! Catch me! Catch me!" the boy calls.

He is running, fast. The rod drops from her hands. The boy's foot catches on something, and then he seems to travel a long, long way. The au pair is finding her feet, trying to stand and turn all at once. The boy feels a chill. Suddenly her arms are there, enfolding him as he knew they would. He flops down and giggles on her shoulder.

"Surprise!" he yells.

But she isn't laughing.

The boy goes silent. Beyond the safety of her shoulder, he detects danger. Beyond her, there is nothing. Only deep water and mud that is deeper than two grown men.

"Oh, my baby," the au pair whispers. "There, there."

She rocks him, and he rests his head on her shoulder for a long time, feeling her chest fall and rise. She kisses the silk of his hair; his eyelashes brush against her collarbone. The au pair holds him until their heartbeats slow and a woman's voice calls out the boy's name. Then she carries him back up to the lighted house and gives him to his mama.

Love in the Tall Grass

Cordelia wakes on a frosty afternoon, watches turf smoke drifting past her bedroom window. She rises, opens the window, and hears the swoon of matinee music in the road. Winter air teems in, on this, the last day of the twentieth century. Cordelia strips naked, pours water from the steel jug, half fills the basin, wrings out the washcloth, and soaps her hands, her face. When the pipes burst in November, she didn't bother with a plumber, broke the ice in the rain barrel and dipped the bucket down. This water's cold. She dries herself and dresses, slowly, in a green dress, fastens the chain of a platinum locket around her neck. She bends and laces up her black shoes, knowing that when this day is over, nothing will ever be the same.

In the kitchen she lowers a bantam's egg into a saucepan, puts the kettle on, takes out the stainless-steel eggcup, its tarnished spoon, the stripy mug and plate, and waits until it's ready. Somewhere somebody is chopping wood. This kettle always sings before it boils. She undoes the bolt and sits beside the open door. She's slept; now she must eat. She breaks the shell, salts the egg, spreads butter over bread, pours tea. The wind blows withered leaves across the linoleum. The Burmese believe that wind carrying betel leaves into the bride's house will bring bad luck and unhappiness to the married couple. So many useless facts rattle like old currency inside Cordelia's head. The clock on the mantel ticks happily. Not long now, it seems to say. Not long now. When she's finished, she turns the eggshell upside down, a trick she played in childhood that turned to habit. She takes a handkerchief from her sleeve and wipes her mouth. It is time. She undoes her braid and brushes out her hair. She knows no other woman whose hair's turned white at forty. Finally, she takes her good black coat from its crook and goes out into what's left of December.

It's been nine years since Cordelia walked this road, a steep road leading to the ocean. Not much has changed. The national school's been painted, but the Silver Dollar Take-Away is still there and the ice-cream van with its sign well faded, but there's a light at the Lone Star Guest house and the little souvenir shop's door is open. She suspects that after the new century's ushered in, they'll close again, wait for summer's tourists and the trampoline kids. She becomes aware of faces behind net curtains. A boy freewheels past her on his bike. She stops at the chapel, slides back the glass door, blesses herself at the font. The porch smells of wet marble, old stone, damp coats. She used to imagine standing here in a wedding dress with her father giving her away.

Inside, the chapel's empty; the marble railing she remembered, gone. Two statues guard the altar: the Virgin Mary and Saint Joseph. One in brown, the other blue. Why is Mary always blue? she wonders. She lights a candle at her feet, she looks so lonely. Near the altar stands a coffin covered in purple cloth, such a small coffin, but then she realizes it's the organ. She backs down into the empty confession box, slides the grid across.

"Bless me, Father, for I have sinned," she whispers.

That takes her back. A sudden draft travels through the chapel, sounding strangely like a motor race, a high revving wind. She sits in the bottom pew and opens the missal at random, reads the lesson from Palm Sunday and thinks Judas Iscariot a beautiful name.

Gorse shelters this road, green, shuddering gorse that bursts into relentless yellow for half the year. It is already getting dark; she feels the light draining, watches the blue dusk setting in the west. She stops and empties a pebble from her shoe. Clouds gather over the barren dunes. She feels her heart beating, feels tired, bone tired, and evening deepens all around her so very quickly. Why does time go fast, then slow? She has to walk two miles or more. She remembers the waiting room, the gleam of the stethoscope, the promise, and hurries on.

So too was it dusk when Cordelia met the doctor, a late September of fallen fruit. Exasperated, she'd taken a hammer and nailed a sign, APPLES, to the front gate. A gale had come during the night and shaken the trees bare. She'd woken and found the orchard grounds carpeted with apples: Granny Smith, Golden Delicious, Bramley, Red Janets, crab apples. She filled buckets, basins, the old Moses basket, but the surplus lay abundant and bruised in the long grass.

When the doctor's car turned into her driveway, Cordelia was sitting on the steps outside her front door, turning the "Jams & Jellies" pages of her cookbook. On the window ledge above her head stood jam jars of drowned wasps, fooled by the spoonful of jam at the bottom of the water. The doctor threw a tall and steady shadow over her. He looked like a man who could jump a fence and climb a tree, like a man who used to run. She led him up the orchard path, where he took his hands out of his pockets and shook his head.

"Such waste," he said. "There's nothing I hate more than waste. Do you have a spade?"

He took his jacket off and rolled up his sleeves. His arms were pale for summer, the veins in his wrists like blue branches a child might draw on a white page. But his hands were tanned, as though he had dipped them in permanent ink that wouldn't wash off. The autumn sun burned orange while the doctor dug a pit. They lined the clay with straw and carefully laid the apples down so they would not touch.

"There," he said, "apples year-round."

"Come in and wash your hands."

Her kitchen was dark and cool and smelled of soot and something else the doctor could not name. Cordelia gave him washing-up liquid, and he stood at the sink scrubbing his hands. She filled a cup with milk, which he drank before he left with a shallow basin full of apples. Cordelia gathered her skirt into a pouch and filled that too. The doctor noticed her knees, marked where she had knelt on the grass, her brown thighs, and thought of them as he drove back home to his wife and children. Every time he turned a bend, the apples rolled around, noisy on the backseat.

The doctor came back. He returned the basin, refilled it at Cordelia's insistence, and returned again. It became habitual, on Thursdays, for the doctor to stop.

"I thought apples were supposed to keep the doctor away," she said.

"Doctors differ."

"And patients?"

"Patients are all the same. Patients just want to feel better."

When the weather was dry, Cordelia and the doctor drank tea outdoors. They sat in the dappled shade beneath the trees, talking. Cordelia asked him about medical school, about being an only child. Neither one of them had a sibling or a living parent. Cordelia was a good listener, and the doctor liked to talk. He talked about his childhood, how he used to stand for hours in the porch killing flies, how his father took more photos of his show dogs than of him, how his aunt was in the convent and his parents had hopes of him joining the priesthood. But he never once mentioned his wife; he was like a book whose middle chapters were missing. Cordelia sensed neglect. Up close, she smelled mothballs in his winter jacket, reminding her of a drawer that hadn't been opened in a very long time.

On her thirtieth birthday, Cordelia sat with her feet in a basin of hot water and listened to the thunderstorm. It was late November. She drank three big vodkas and tied a ribbon in her hair. Lightning flashed across the room. When the doctor arrived, she took his hand and led him out to the orchard. She lay down on the wet grass.

"I'm thirty," she said.

"You'll catch cold."

"I don't care."

"Are you drunk?"

"Does it matter?" she said, and unbuttoned her dress.

They lost track of time. When the doctor looked at the time, he had put the face of his watch up close to his, then rushed off, leaving skid marks in the avenue.

The next morning Cordelia lay in bed while drowsy bluebottles struggled against the windowpanes. She watched the sudden, fast shadows of swallows who flew past her window in fleeting pairs subtracting light from her room and marveled how living things could suspend themselves in midair. She imagined the last of the overripe fruit, the latecomers, falling in the slightest breeze. She did not have the heart to pluck them. She imagined the stem weakening, the fruit clinging to its source, losing, loosening, then letting go, falling.

The doctor told his wife he was out on house calls. Because his car was so conspicuous, they started to meet on the sand dunes at Strandhill. They brought drumsticks, a flask of whiskey, cake, and bars of Belgian chocolate because the doctor had a sweet tooth. On dry days, he opened his shirt and she kicked her boots off and let her hair down. But mostly they just lay there with Cordelia's

[48]

big black coat over them, listening to the tide, he with his head in the reeds. Sometimes they fell into shallow sleep, but always Cordelia was aware of the irreversible ticking of the doctor's gold watch: tick, tick, tick. Not long now, it seemed to say. Not long now. She hated that watch; she wanted to stand up and throw it in the ocean.

Cordelia dreamt she was in a room with a green, flapping curtain. She could see out, but nobody could see in. When she told the doctor of this, he started talking about his wife. Cordelia didn't want to know about his wife. She wanted him to bang on her door in the middle of the night with his fist, to come in with a suitcase and call her by her name and say, "I've come to live with you at my own peril." She wanted him to carry her into a strange house and leave the door wide open. The doctor said his wife went to bed early. He said on fine nights he sat out on the stoop behind his house and smoked a cigarette. From there he could see the headland farther up, where the road curved into the lights of her village.

Winter came with sudden, unpredictable showers. Cordelia met him in pubs, where they ate red meat and wine. It was dark by four o'clock, and the doctor talked about getting married, how he'd felt that it was something he had to do, so he married the first woman who would have him, at twenty-two. He had no sense of himself. His wife gave up her job and got pregnant. She couldn't sew. If a button went missing from his shirt, she threw it out. Cordelia didn't ask why he didn't sew on his own buttons.

They got away for a weekend in Dublin. She met him in the local town, and he told her to lie down in the backseat of the car until they got away on the main road. When they reached the hotel, his solicitor was standing at the reception desk. The doctor introduced Cordelia as his colleague. He stank of guilt. They made love with the window open, listening to the Liffey flowing down Eden Quay. It felt good to be surrounded by strangers. The doctor went to his meetings in the afternoons, found quiet restaurants at night. He was careful with his money, talked about the price of sterling, how his wife bought a coat for £300 without consulting him. Once Cordelia came out of the bathroom and found him looking through her handbag.

"Any aspirin?" he asked. "I've a headache."

On Christmas week, he came to her house with steaks and served them up half raw with a bottle of brandy.

"Happy Christmas," he said and gave her a box of dark chocolates. She was allergic to chocolate.

She didn't see him for two weeks afterwards. He called her from the phone box at two A.M.

"Where were you when I was twenty?" he said. His speech was slurred. "My wife wants to know why I don't touch her. It's like touching a snake. She's going home to Kilkenny for the weekend. She's taking the kids. Where do you want to go?"

"Spain."

"Right! Ha! Ha! Spain it is!"

That weekend he took Cordelia to a town in Limerick whose only industry was its abattoir. There was a rancid smell in that town, and they got a room in a hotel whose hot taps never got hotter than lukewarm. A tinker's wedding reception was in full swing downstairs. Cordelia got drunk. She walked down the corridor in her nightdress. The wool carpet under her feet depicted huge red roses. She stood at the window looking at the married couple going away in a buggy drawn by donkeys. People threw flowers and beer cans at the limousine.

"'Til death does us part," the doctor said. "It's always married people who cry at weddings. They know the difference between the vows and the life."

They gave each other things. That was their first mistake. He took a pair of surgical scissors from his pocket and snipped off a lock of Cordelia's hair. He kept this between the pages of a book named *Doctor Zhivago*. Another time, having lain out in the dunes past dark, they accidentally wore each other's scarves home. He gave her old books whose pages were edged in gold. And Cordelia wrote long letters on white pages saying days without him were like months without a sunrise, without oxygen.

In the middle of the night, while his wife and children slept, the doctor climbed high up above the drawing room, pushed the attic door open, and placed the things Cordelia had given him under the insulation. He knew they would be safe there, for his wife was afraid of heights.

But the doctor never wrote a line to Cordelia. When he went away to Lisbon on vacation with his wife, Cordelia received no word from him, not even a postcard. The only specimen of his handwriting she'd ever witnessed was when he gave her painkillers for an earache. Across the label in an almost illegible hand was written: "One to be taken with water (or vodka) three times daily."

Cordelia is almost there. She passes concrete railings at the car park, climbs the steep incline through the dunes, under the shadow of the mountain. She stands to get her breath back, watches the toss and turn of the blue-bellied tide breaking into perpetual, salty lather on the strand. Reeds bend low to let the wind pass. There's little to show human presence here; the wind has rubbed all footprints from the sand. Just a broken plastic spoon, a buckled beer can, a child's beaded purse. Cordelia stops and stoops to pick it up, but it's empty, its lining torn.

Lights from the town throw an orange sash across the east. She hears music, tinkers playing Jim Reeves records on the halting site, the systematic purr of a generator. A piebald mare whinnies and canters down along the ocean's edge as if she too has dreamt of a man holding a gun to her head. Clouds accumulate, thicken in the darkness. Cordelia finds the mossy patch on the hill where they first lay down. That was almost ten years ago. She lies in the reeds, pulls her collar up, and waits.

The doctor walked into his drawing room one afternoon, and there on the floor was the piece of black ribbon he'd taken from Cordelia's hair to bundle up her letters, each one addressed to his surgery and marked "strictly confidential." When he raised his head, he saw his wife's legs dangling over the edge of the ceiling.

"Whose hair is this? Who sent these letters? Who have you been seeing? Who owns this ribbon? Who? I want to know; speak to me. Who is Cordelia? Cordelia who?"

His wife read aloud. She began to cry. There were words like "forever," "always," and "'til death does us part." It was late afternoon when she began. The doctor sat in the armchair by the fire and through the window watched the shuddering chrysanthemums pressing their rust-colored blooms against the panes. His wife dropped each page to the living room floor as she read. These pages floated, and by the time she'd finished, she had asked for a flashlight to read by. At the end of many pages was written, in a generous hand, the name Cordelia. The doctor's wife would not come down but sat there, insisting on the truth.

"Are you in love with her?"

"In love?" asked the doctor in an astonished voice.

"She's obviously in love with you."

"It's infatuation, nothing more."

"You think I'm dull as ditch water. You'll leave me."

"Don't be ridiculous. You're my wife."

He lured her down. A splendid fire throve in the hearth, for the doctor, out of nerves, had thrown shovelfuls of coal onto the flames. Before dawn, in the presence of her husband, she slowly burned Cordelia's letters. The doctor watched the fire devouring the pages, Cordelia's lock of milky hair singeing in the blue heat. He thought about the burns he'd treated, the very worst cases, and yet it took all his strength not to put his hands into the flames to retrieve them.

"She's blond," said the doctor's wife.

Two days later the doctor called Cordelia into his surgery and in a low, sensitive voice, informed her that their affair was over. He joined his hands and pushed his thumbs around in small, anticlockwise circles. This must be what it's like to be informed of a terminal illness, she thought. He talked and talked, but at some point Cordelia stopped listening. She was reading the eye-test chart behind his head. She couldn't read the small print at the bottom. Maybe she needed glasses.

The doctor put his head in his hands.

"Oh Cordelia," he said, "I can't leave her. You know I can't. Think of the children. Think of them asking, 'Where's Daddy?'"

"Where's Daddy?" For a reason unknown to her, she felt like laughing.

"Wait for me," he said. "In ten years' time the children will be grown and gone. Meet me on New Year's Eve at the turn of the century. Meet me then, and I will come home and live with you," he said. "I promise! You'll haunt me 'til then."

Cordelia laughed, and that was the last she saw of him. She passed patients in the waiting room. The snively middle-aged woman with the tissues, the pale man with his bandaged arm, the wounded? Was everybody waiting for this man?

Gradually, the bad dream faded. The green curtain and the window furled backwards into memory, but the promise stoked like a hot poker in Cordelia's head. Cordelia coveted her solitude. She started reading late into the night, playing her piano, practicing uncomplicated airs. She talked to herself, speaking freely in the empty rooms. She didn't make any sense. Slowly she became a recluse. She covered the TV with a tablecloth and put a vase of flowers there; she threw the transistor radio with all its bad news away. She made lists, paid her bills through the mail. She got the phone in, realized the turf man, the grocer, the gas man, anyone she wanted, would call around and deliver. They left cardboard boxes full of groceries, gas cylinders, and bags of turf outside the door, took the checks from under the stone. She rose late, drank strong tea, made a ritual of cleaning out the grates. She grew thin and stopped attending mass. Neighbors knocked on her door and peered in through the windows, but she did not answer. A powder of rust-colored ash fell over the house, accumulated on every horizontal surface. It seemed that every time she moved, dust rose.

Evenings, she lit the fire, watched the whoosh of flame around the turf, and listened to the rhododendron hedge, the Virginia creeper scratching the windowpanes. Cordelia imagined someone out there in the dark, rubbing a peephole in the dirty glass to see in, but she knew it was only the hedge. She had always kept the garden, stayed out in summer with the clippers, trimmed it all back and raked the laurel leaves off the sandy path, mowed the grass, lit small, inoffensive fires whose smoke poured down beyond the clothesline. Now the neglected hedge began to intrude upon the house, grew so thick and close that it kept all the downstairs rooms in constant shadow, and when the sun was going down, strange, monkey-puzzle shadows poured into the sitting room. Cordelia could sit under the reading lamp in the middle of the day and pretend it was night. Time didn't seem to matter. Years passed. Sometimes, when the weather was warm and the rhododendron buds opened, she walked naked around the house, brushing against the damp blooms. Nobody ever saw her.

It is night now at Strandhill. The half moon seems to throw more light than it should. Cordelia can discern the outline of the cliffs against the sky. The ocean is as it always was; the childish notion occurs to her that the waves say he loves me, he loves me not. It is a terrible thing to be a fool at forty. She has been alone too long. Nothing and everything has changed. Cordelia feels she has run a very long race, and now her heartbeat may slow down to normal. One way or the other, this is the end. She puts her hand to her face, takes comfort in the warmth of her breath. She feels the wind getting colder, pulls her coat around her, fastens her buttons. It won't be long now. She closes her eyes, remembers the snip of his scissors cutting her hair, hot, broken sleep, a green bruise fading on her neck, lying down on the back seat of his car, the eye chart in the surgery.

A small parade marches across the hill, holding torches, gearing up for midnight. It is the brass, trumpet music of people celebrating the passage of time. A boy in costume beats a drum. They march in their own time. Girls in mini-skirts are twirling batons, making for the lights of town.

"Cordelia." A woman stands over her. "You don't know me. You knew my husband; he was the doctor," she says.

Was the doctor? *Was?*

"The doctor won't be coming."

Cordelia is startled. It is a long time since she has spoken to another human. She doesn't know what to say.

"You didn't think I knew?"

The doctor's wife is a lithe, small woman with a lot of white in her eyes. She pulls the belt of her coat tight around her waist as if to make it smaller.

"It was obvious. When your husband comes home from house calls with sand in his shoes, his shirt buttons done up wrong, hair brushed, smelling of mints, and a gigantic appetite, you don't have to be a genius to figure out what's going on." She takes out cigarettes and offers one to Cordelia. Cordelia shakes her head, watches the face in the flame of the lighter. It is the face of a woman who was once good looking, but there's desperation there now.

"You write beautiful letters. I have never in my life received a letter such as yours." The drum is beating faintly now on the headland. "You know the funniest thing? The funniest thing is, I used to pray he'd leave me. I used to get down on my knees and say the rosary so he'd leave me. He kept your letters and things in the attic; I used to hear him up there at night, getting the ladder. He must have thought I was deaf. Anyway, I was sure he'd leave me when I discovered them. He loved you as much as he is capable of love. It's no consolation, but I'm sure of that."

"Loved?"

"I didn't have the heart to leave him, nor he, me. We were cowards." Her voice is breaking. She looks out toward the ocean and composes herself. "Look at your hair. Your hair's white. What age are you?"

"Just forty."

The doctor's wife shakes her head, reaches out, touches Cordelia's hair.

"I feel like I'm a hundred."

"I know."

The doctor's wife lies down in the reeds and smokes. Cordelia feels no ill will toward this woman, none of the biting envy she imagined.

"How did you know I'd be here?"

"He has a terrible memory, writes everything down. And he believes his handwriting is illegible. You're penciled in. 'C. Strandhill at midnight.'"

"Strandhill at midnight."

"Not very romantic, is it? You'd think he'd remember."

The tinkers' fire in the car park is sending out the smell of burning rubber when the doctor runs up the dunes.

"I took a wild guess," says the doctor's wife.

He stands there, looking ten years older and out of breath. In the moonlight, his suit is shiny. He is alive, and it is almost midnight. Cordelia is pleased, but nothing is as she imagined. The doctor does not reach out for her. He does not lie down in the tall grass and put his head in the crook of her arm, as he used. He stands there as if he has arrived too late at the scene of an accident, knowing he might have done something if only he had come earlier. Behind their backs the perpetual noise of the ocean folds in on itself. Together they listen to the tide, the contradictory waves, counting down what time remains. Because they don't know what to say or do, they do and say nothing. All three of them just sit there, waiting: Cordelia, the doctor, and his wife, all three mortals waiting, waiting for somebody to leave.

Storms

My mother dreamt things before they happened and found things in her dreams. I was at the kitchen table cutting doors and windows out of a cardboard box the morning she came downstairs and said she knew where Rua was. She was in a hurry.

"I'm coming!"

"Be quick if you are."

It was one of those frosty mornings in the middle of January when the air is so cold it feels new. When we stepped outside, the wind shocked the breath back into my lungs. I followed her down the lane, into the wood. A woodcock flew up over the trees. Something told me I shouldn't talk. My mother knew where she was going. We crossed a ditch and came out in a beet field I didn't recognize. She stopped and pointed at a clump of briars.

"He's in there," she said.

We pulled back the briars, and there was Rua, our red setter, with his neck caught in a snare. He looked dead, but I couldn't look away. My mother loosened the snare and talked to him. There was blood on the wire. We carried him home and gave him milk, but he couldn't swallow. Bones stuck out through his coat, and he slept for three days. On the fourth day he got up and followed my mother like a shadow around the house. When I asked her if I too would find things in my dreams, she said she hoped that would never happen. I did not ask why. Even though I was a child, I had long since learned that *why* was a word my mother hated.

The dairy was a cool, dark room my parents filled with the things they seldom used, from the time before I was born. Yellow paint bubbled on the walls, and damp flagstones shone across the floor. Bridles hung stiff on the beams, their bits dusty. The churn was still there and the smell of the sour milk still in it, the wood smooth but riddled with woodworm, the paddles long since lost. I never remember glass in those windows, only rusted bars and the strange applause of the wind blowing in through the trees.

Someone shoved the old incubator into the dairy and a chicken run, a rusted, metal affair that used to shine like teaspoons. We would put newly hatched chickens in there, scoop them up in our hands like yellow petals and drop them into that heat, the fluffy balls with legs always moving, taking in that warmth as their own. Warmth keeps us alive. Sometimes those yellow balls fell down, the cold inside winning over, the feet like orange arrows pointing down. My father's hand chucked them out like young weeds. My mother's picked them gently, inspecting those yellow bodies for some sign of life, and finding none, she'd say: "My poor chicken," and smile at me as she slid them down the chute.

Claire Keegan

The milk strainers were still there too, the old gauze hanging in dirty clumps on a fraying thread. And the jars of gooseberry jam that smelled like sherry, shrunken in the glass with the whisker of mold. My mother always made more jam than we could eat. We used to make crab-apple jelly, quarter those sour fruits and boil them to a pulp, cores and seeds and all. Poured the lumpy fluid into an old pillowcase, a corner on each leg of a stool turned upside down. Drip, drip, drip into the preserving pot all night.

I went into the dairy when I was sent—for a pot of varnish, six-inch nails, a bridle for a mare whose head was big. The latch was too high. I had to stand on a can of creosote to reach up, and the metal round I pressed on was leaf thin. When I went there of my own accord, it was to look into the chest, a big rusted box, a pirate's suitcase to a child. It was so old that if you emptied it out and held it up to the light, it would be like looking through a colander. There was nothing in it I liked—old books stuck together with damp, no pictures, brown maps, and some prayer books.

"It all belonged to your father's people," my mother told me, using the voice he was not supposed to hear.

The chest was just as long as me and half as tall, with a tight lid and no handles. I would open it and look at those things, finger the books with their fractured spines, the missing covers. It was the past; the past was in there. I felt that if I could understand its contents, my life would make more sense. But that never happened. I would get fed up looking at those things, slam the lid down hard, make that metal screech.

[62]

The next dream changed everything. My mother dreamt of her mother, dead. Her wailing woke me in the middle of the night. Someone was banging the kitchen table. I stole downstairs and stood there watching through the dark. My mother was curled up on the floor. My father, who never spoke a tender word, was speaking tender words, coaxing her with brandy, saying her name.

"Mary, Mayree, ah Maayree!"

The two people who never touched, whose fingers left the gravy jug before the other's clasp, were touching. I crept back upstairs and listened as those tender words changed into something else.

Morning brought the telegram. The postman took his cap off and told my mother he was sorry for her troubles. My mother rolled the telegram between her fingers like a cigarette paper. My father made arrangements. Strangers came into the house. A neighboring woman's hand slapped mine when it turned the wireless on. My grandmother, the woman with the purple rash and the blue-veined breasts we had washed like a painting, came back stiff from the old folks' home in a frill-lined box, and we put her in the cool of the parlor. I got up in the middle of the night and went down to see her when nobody was there. A draft blew grease from the lighted candle across the top of the sideboard. I knew little about her, except that she was not afraid of hissing geese or of catching TB. She could cure any ailment in fowl. My mother had grown up surrounded by ducks and hens and turkeys. I touched my grandmother's hand. The cold frightened me.

Claire Keegan

"What do you think you're doing?" my mother asked.

She had been sitting there all the time in the dark.

"Nothing," I said.

Neighbors came in a convoy after the funeral, cars bumper to bumper in the lane. I sat on strangers' laps. They passed me around like the tobacco pouch, and I drank three big bottles of 7-Up.

My aunt stood guarding the ham. "Who's for another nice bit of center cut then?" the carving knife deadly in her hand.

My mother sat staring into the fire and never said a word. Not even when Rua got up on the chaise longue and licked himself.

Months passed. My mother took to cleaning out the cow house, even though we had sold the cows years back. She went out with the yard brush and the bucket, scrubbed the stalls, the aisle, even shone the old hubcap we'd used to pour frothy milk into for the cats. And then she came inside and talked to the statues until dinnertime. She imagined storms, locked herself under the stairs when she heard wind, put cotton wool in her ears when the thunder came, hid under the table with Rua.

Once my father and I, rolling barley in the loft, watched her calling up the field to the cows.

"Chuck! Chuck! Hersey! Chuck! Hersey!" She stood there rattling the zinc bucket to bring the imaginary cows down for their feed. My father took her inside. And that was when my mother started living upstairs.

So when summer came, I was the one who carried out the big teapot to the hay makers, the spout plugged with a page from the *Farmer's Journal*. The men sucked their tráithníns and watched me and told my father with full mouths that I would soon be old enough.

She came for me in the middle of the night wearing a red nightdress I had never seen. She pulled me out of bed, down the stairs in the dark, and out through the mown meadow, past the cocks of hay, our bare feet picking up the seed. Up and up we went through the stubble fields, her hand a vise grip, the tail of her nightie whipping out behind her in the wind. And then we reached the top of the top and lay down on our backs, watching the stars, she with her brassy hair and mad words, not senseless at all, but sensing what we couldn't. The way the dog is the first to hear the car in the lane.

She pointed out what she called the saucepan, an arrangement of stars, and told me how it came to be there. It was a story about animals during the time of Our Lord, in Africa. A drought came. The ground was dust, even the riverbeds ran dry. Animals roamed around Africa looking for a drink. Sheep lost their wool, and snakes their skins, but a young sow found a saucepan full of water and gave them all a drink to tide them over until it rained. All the animals drank their fill, but the saucepan never dried out. It had a crooked handle, and when the rain came, the stars took on its shape, and that's what was up there. And then I too could see it in the sky.

Claire Keegan

We stayed there until dawn, the smell of hay coming up on the wind. She told me about my father, how he'd bruised her for fifteen years, because she was not the same as other women. She taught me the difference between loving and liking somebody. She said she didn't like me any more than him because I had the same, cruel eyes.

I didn't understand, but that is when I started going into the dairy without being sent. It was a quiet room. There was nothing, only the wind blowing in and the gurgling of the water tank overhead. The hole in the ceiling between the beams showed the playhouse, the place where my cousins used to take their dolls apart and hit their heads on the sloping roof.

It was a stormy day, the day the van came to take her away. My father said she was hurting but it wasn't anything you could see. I asked him if he meant she was bleeding on the inside.

"Something like that," he said.

I thought of the sacred heart picture over the stove, the red exposed heart lit by the red lamp that never went out.

Men are coming into the house to get her. She's under the table. I can't watch. I run to the dairy, open the chest and look inside. I pick up a prayer book and finger the leaves. They are tan and smooth like my mother's arm. I open one of the torn, brown maps, and, until I find a place I recognize, I cannot discern which is the land and which the sea. The wing of an insect is stuck to Norway. I can hear them in the next room. I open another book and look for pictures, but there are none. I get into the chest, squat

[66]

down. I hear glass breaking. The sound of what has become my mother's voice rises to a wail. Something falls. I pull the tin roof, let that metal fall in over me with a rusty, tightening screech. Everything turns black. It is as if I no longer exist. It is not me sitting on the damp books inside a big, black tin. The smell is old and musty like the smell in the bread bin or the back of the cupboard where the cake crumbs stay. A smell that's a century old. I remember rats ate through the grid of the incubator once. They got at the chickens, and we found pieces of fluff everywhere with legs attached, the fleshy bodies eaten out. We found others terrified, exhausted, and hiding between cans of paint or rolls of sheepwire, unable as yet to fly away. We picked them up, their yellow bodies throbbing, tiny bellows gone mad.

I run the house now. The last man who said I was old enough got scalded. My mother always said there was nothing as bad as a burn. And she was right. It's turning out that I'm taking no nonsense from anybody. They leave their Wellingtons outside the door, and my father leaves his dirty dishes on the draining board. I haven't heard him say the spuds are hard in the middle. I'd lash with the serving spoon. He knows that too. Rua goes around the house looking for her. I think of him as my mother's shadow, roaming the house.

I visit her on Sundays, but she doesn't know where she is or who I am.

"It's me, Mam," I say.

"I never could stand the smell of fish," she says. "Him and his herrings."

"Do you not know me? It's Ellen."

"Ellen of Troy! Get on yer horse!" she says.

She's clever at cards, cheats the other ones out of their pocket money every week, and the matron has to go and fish it out of her locker while she's in the bath. She doesn't miss it. Money never held any interest for my mother.

But I keep going back to the loony bin. I like the smell of disinfectant in the corridors, the nurses' rubber-soled shoes, the quarreling over Sunday newspapers. I like the way their conversation makes no sense. What does that say about me? Mother always said madness ran in families, and I have it from the two sides. I live in a house with the man my mother married. I have a dog who almost died but doesn't care about being alive. When I look at myself in the mirror, my eyes are cruel.

I suppose I've my own reasons for coming here. Maybe I need a little of what my mother has. Just a little. I take a small share of it for my own protection. It is like a vaccination. People don't understand, but you have to face the worst possible case to be able for anything.

Ride If You Dare

Roslin pulls into the Gator Lodge parking lot and puts on the hand brake. The signs are good; nobody around. Just a couple of cars parked out back, an old blue Buick standing next to a chipped pickup with an ugly brown mutt panting in the cab. She hopes it isn't his. They say a man picks out a dog that's just like him, and this dog is ugly.

She steps out into the heat, smells fish in the garbage. Lunch is well over. She brushes the creases from her skirt and takes a deep breath and walks the gravel in her high heels. A fat lizard zigzags across the stucco. She swings the door open, feels the blast of cold off the air conditioner.

"I'll be the guy in the blue shirt," he'd said.

"Every second guy in the world has a blue shirt—wear a hat."

"That won't make no difference; every second guy in Mississippi wears a hat anyhow."

"Just wear it," she'd said.

A waitress is smoothing out a bundle of dollar bills at the bar. She stubs out her cigarette when she sees Roslin and gives her a four o'clock smile. A guy wearing a blue shirt is sitting by the windows with his back to her. There's

[69]

a cowboy hat on his table. He's the only customer in the place. Roslin walks right up to him.

"You Guthrie?"

"That's me. You're Roslin?"

She nods.

"'Fraid I got tired of wearing the hat." He gestures to his head, stupid, like she wouldn't know where a hat went. He'd planned to stand up and pull out her chair, show some manners, but Roslin's sitting down already, hooking the plastic strap of her purse over the back of her seat. She's a lot prettier than he expected. He thought she'd be a fat girl with that telephone laugh.

She thinks he must have done this before. He's cool headed, his face is smooth as chrome, dented below the cheekbones. Nothing to say this isn't just a casual meeting between two friends, that she isn't just some lady who's strolled in and sat down beside him because there's nobody else in the place and she needs a little company. But they aren't too concerned. Chances are, if somebody they know does walk in, they won't be honeymooners, lunching on this blue shift. All that thinking and talking for too long over the phone and now they're here, taking a chance, sitting opposite one another in a Mississippi watering hole with nothing to hold on to. Damn.

"I was thinking maybe you'd changed your mind," he says, placing his palm down flat on the oilcloth. His nails are long. A band of pale skin stands out on his third finger. "You want a drink or something?"

[70]

"Hell, yeah. You eaten?" She pulls the red napkin out of her glass and spreads it out on her lap.

"Naw. I was holding out for you."

He holds his menu up between them like a shield and chooses his words.

"You like seafood?"

"Sure I like seafood. What you think I am? Jewish?"

He doesn't have anything to say to that.

"Jesus, are you Jewish?"

He laughs. "You the prettiest thing I seen in a long time," he says, thinking it sounds like a bad line when he hears it out loud. He'd rehearsed his lines all the way over, damn near rear-ended a Corvette, and here he is saying the oldest words in the book but meaning it. This woman smells good. She's blond and tanned, with a good figure, even if she is too smart to be a real windfall. She pouts and looks down at the menu. There's black mascara on her eyelashes, blue shadow on the lids; he can see how dark her hair is at the roots.

They read the courses on the menu, their eyes roving over the dishes, all the hors d'oeuvres, the entrées, the dessert menu on the back, and the different beers from all over the world from the drinks page. Roslin could go for a big fat slice of that devil's food cake, but the hook on her brassiere is pinching her back as it is. She hasn't worn it since they had Nelson's youngster christened up in Mobile. Guthrie thinks he better order something without garlic.

The waitress comes over and takes a pencil from behind her ear.

Claire Keegan

"You folks ready?"

She keeps her eyes on the cowboy hat while she takes their orders. It's a great big hat with a Saints button pinned into the band. Raw oysters and dirty rice with another Bud for the cowboy. Boiled crawfish for the lady, and scotch, straight up.

"You ain't driving?" he asks.

"No. I got here on a white mule."

"The lady's got a sense of humor. I like that."

"Glad you approve."

He blushes and looks out the window. The restaurant stands on stilts over the water, the muddy backwash breaking against the poles that are holding them up. The sun's so bright, he can hardly see, as if it's having a big orgy in the sky and blinds every eye so nobody can know what's really going on up there. That's what he's thinking when the waitress brings the drinks and crackers.

They light cigarettes because there's nothing else to say. Just a few words and it's all opened up. It's as if she's slid the zipper of his pants down. She can't believe she's driven all the way out here to meet up with a guy she's never laid eyes on. One little ad placed in the *Times Picayune*, a WOMAN WANTED in bold, a few phone calls, and this. The fact that they're here says everything, and now that they've seen each other, it's done.

She takes out a Marlboro. He flicks the lid off his lighter and holds out the flame. She lowers her head and exhales through her nose, looking at him. He thinks she's like one of them movie stars, like Lauren Bacall or Madonna or

[72]

somebody, with those fancy clothes and those long fin-
gernails. She downs her scotch before the food arrives,
leaving a thick smear of lipstick on the glass. He wishes
he could tell the guys down at the mill about this. Big
Andy could put that in his lunch box, but Big Andy can't
hold his own water after two beers. He starts on the crackers, snatches off the plastic wrappers, and gulps his beer.

"When's the last time you ate?"

"Yesterday," he says.

When the food arrives, Roslin handles her crawfish like
china and sucks the heads, throws the shells on the side
and drinks her second scotch. Guthrie piles forkfuls of
dirty rice on his crackers, squeezes lemon juice and
Tabasco on the oysters, slurps them down.

"You want me to make you one?" he asks.

"Uh-uh. I don't eat anything that's raw. You want one
of these?" she asks, holding a crawfish by the claw.
"They're real good. Spicy."

"Nah, if I start eating those things, I'll never stop. Like
cookies."

"And affairs."

He straightens up. "Ain't true," he says. "I ain't never
done this before."

"First time for everything, I guess. You placed that ad
out of desperation, then, huh? Of course, if that's the case,
I'm responding to desperation—don't say much for me
now, does it?"

"Guess we've got something in common."

"I never said I was desperate—I said you was."

[73]

"You just doing a survey then, huh?"

She laughs.

The cook pushes through the swinging doors from the kitchen. He's damp around the armpits. When he goes out onto the porch, a blast of hot air swings into the room. They can feel the temperature rising.

Guthrie starts talking, tells Roslin about working down at the mill, the way Lardhead got his hand caught in the saw 'cause it was where it shouldn't have been, how he collected all of that insurance money but it was his right hand and he was right handed. Roslin tells about how she painted the whole shotgun apartment, every room eggshell blue, couldn't get the paint out of her hair for weeks, about that time she broke down on the highway and made a fan belt out of her panty hose. They skirt the conversation around their home lives, each trying to peer into the other's kitchen window without making it obvious, wondering if there's a high chair in there.

They order another one after the dishes are taken away, and one more before he pays the bill. Roslin watches him peeling the bills off a roll.

"You didn't get nothing caught in a saw, did ya?"

"No, ma'am. All my bodily parts function just fine."

He pulls out her chair. The waitress yawns as she collects the glasses and the five-dollar tip. When they bang the screen door, they disturb the cook having his snooze on the porch before dinner. He hears them talking about whose car they'll take, but he doesn't bother opening his eyes to see which direction they drive off in.

They take Roslin's truck, drive down through rodeo territory, past Picayune, and on toward Jackson. They don't have any idea where they're going or when they'll stop. Roslin weaves in and out between the lanes, as if driving away from home will push that feeling farther away too. But the farther she drives, the bigger that feeling grows. Roslin's not dumb. She knows she's driving 'cause she has something to drive away from.

They talk for a bit, but it turns quiet because they can't think of anything more to say. He wants to put his feet up on the dashboard while she drives, but he keeps them on the floor and smokes his cigarettes, rolls the window down, hoping the breeze will blow his nerves away. Then the silence changes the way it sometimes does, and they're happy not talking. They just watch the signs and the high corn swaying on both sides of the highway, the gleam of the white sun on the hood.

Roslin thinks about her husband. She used to call him her man. My man, she'd say, even when he wasn't around. All looks and cold as a can of beer right out of the icebox, but he has brains about the little things. Can get the whiff of scotch on her breath even when she's brushed her teeth, knows when she buys the étoufée from the store and spices it up when she can't be bothered cooking, even though she pitches the can. The kind of man you don't touch easy. She used to think he was like Robert De Niro or Sean Penn, waters that run deep. She spent ten years with him, trying to get into that place where he lived, because she figured if he went to all that trouble, there

must be something real precious inside, like the pearl
trapped inside the oyster shell. But then she just gave up
and realized there was nothing in there, just a hard, empty
shell. He'd sunk all his energy into building that thing;
then he got into that groove and forgot all about what it
was that he started out protecting. The day she realized
that, she got drunk in the living room, started right after
breakfast on scotch with ice all the way up to the top. As
soon as he came home and saw her lounging in her underwear, panties stuck to her in the heat, sitting in his armchair, air all sluggish, room hot as hell, fans on full blast,
he knew she'd walk. He could tell. And she knew he
could. The day you find out you've just wasted ten years
is no picnic. And she didn't even want to hit him; she
just wanted to kick herself.

"What you thinking?"

She looks at Guthrie. She likes the way his shirt fits him.

"How come they call you Guthrie? I never knowed anybody by that name."

"Oh, Mama was a big Woody Guthrie fan, so she called
me after him. I'm lucky I didn't grow up on a train."

"So Woody Guthrie ain't your daddy then, huh?"

"Damn close."

"Well, Guthrie, you wanna tune a song in on that
radio?"

"Yeah. What you wanna hear?"

"Anything. So long as it ain't glum."

He tunes in the oldies station. Buddy Holly, Ruby
Turner, the Beatles all the way over the bypass and out

the other side. They drown out Aretha Franklin, bawl along with Chuck Berry singing "You Never Can Tell," walk the line with Johnny Cash. Neither one can carry a tune. Guthrie whistles. She never did know anybody to whistle out of tune before. She clicks her fingers in time and her bangles shake for miles. He says it's like driving with Mister Bojangles. She almost says Mrs. Bojangles but shuts her mouth up just in time. She thinks about reaching over and holding his hand and shifting the gears with it the way they did in high school. They stop for gas at the other side of Jackson and hop back in right after they pay the guy and get the six pack, because stopping might mean turning back. They drink Budweiser and buckle up the cans, let them clunk around the floor on the bends.

The traffic slows down, and they turn down the radio to see what's going on. Men in yellow jackets are directing traffic, cars are parked up on the side of the road, far as they can see. Then they see the lights of a Ferris wheel turning on a patch of yellow sunset.

"Carnival! Jesus H. Let's go there!" Guthrie yells, leaning out the passenger window. "Get up on that damn wheel and go way the hell up." He figures they have to stop sometime, and a wet county is better than the desert.

"You wanna?"

"Yeah, I wanna do that. Get on that thing and scare the shit out of myself good." He hasn't ridden one of those things in years.

"You're crazy," she says, but she makes the U-turn and drives into the field. They park the truck and slam the doors shut, lock the keys in the ignition without taking any notice. "It's like Jazz Fest!" Guthrie says.

"Let's get more beer!"

Kids are walking around holding too many things, balloons in one hand, cotton candy in the other. Soft toys under Mama's elbow because Daddy can shoot straight. Guthrie thinks it'd be a good thing if somebody tied a big helium balloon onto every one of those little waistbands, send them all shooting right up into the sky, when the clown comes over. He's wearing one of them red noses and his white, painted face is flaking off. He takes an egg from behind Roslin's ear and a quarter from Guthrie's.

"Now, ain't that clever?" Guthrie says. "How'd you do that?"

"Magic," the clown says.

"Magic, my grandma. That's a neat trick, making money out of thin air."

But "magic" is all the clown will say, so Roslin gives him a dollar bill and he shoves off to the next couple.

They stand under the Ferris wheel sipping beer from plastic cups. The seats are full of people spinning slowly around. Roslin is sick to her stomach just watching them.

"So you wanna go on that wheel?" she asks.

"Damn straight. I'll get us tickets."

"I ain't going," she says, shaking her head.

"What you mean you ain't going?"

"You want me to sing it for you? I'd swallow raw eggs sooner than get up on that thing."

"Aw, come on. We'll get good and scared."

"You go."

"You're coming with me."

"No I ain't."

"Well, if you ain't going, I ain't going neither."

They stroll around the field some more, Roslin's heels sinking in the grass. There are booths with candy and ice cream, stalls jammed full of people putting their money down on their lucky numbers for the fortune wheel, throwing darts, trying to get plastic rings over junk toys. Little fake horses keep making it to the finish post. There's a claw machine with its limp metal claw hanging down over all the plastic junk. They eye a stuffed seal nosing up over the giraffes, put all their quarters in and keep watching the claw drop, but it just slides across those toys every time like its battery's going dead.

"Damn!"

"Not to worry. Ain't the fish we're after," Guthrie says as he puts his last quarter in and watches the claw dip, then rise up, empty.

The waltzer, a big, orange pot with seats, scrambles the riders, their pale faces whizzing past, screaming.

"You wanna take a turn on there?" he asks.

"Uh-uh. I'd just puke up my crawfish. They should call those things the spin and spew."

One bottle-fishing stall is for the over twenty-ones, has bottles of liquor lined up on a table fenced off with rope. The poles holding the rope up are beginning to droop. They take a turn fishing for bottles at three bucks a turn. He eyes a bottle of bourbon, thinking it might come in

handy later on, but the cap is smooth, nothing to catch
on to and the ring at the end of the pole fits tight, so he'd
need a real steady hand. The guy on the end with the big
buckle on his pants wins every time, so the man who
runs the stall tells him to shove off, says he has enough
liquor to throw a party.

They watch riders coming down the slide. A yellow,
plastic chute that dips like a waist in the middle. Must be
over a hundred feet long. People are climbing up the steps
on the other side and sliding right down to the bottom like
crazy on a piece of sack. Monster Slide, the sign at the bottom reads, RIDE IF YOU DARE.

"Let's get on that thing!" Guthrie says.

"No way."

"Aw, come on. Don't you wanna go on one of these
things? We can't come all the way down here and just do
nothing. Show some backbone!"

"I'm scared to death of heights."

"Life needs a little risk, Roslin," he says. "We can go
down together. I won't let nothing happen to you."

She looks at the people sliding down. Screaming kids,
couples, old guys with the waistbands high over their
bellies, out for a good time.

"It's awful high."

He coaxes her up there. He takes her hand, and they
drain their beers and dump the cups on the grass. The
ticket guy on the ground has a bored, New York accent.
He takes the money and hands over the sacks. They get
in line at the foot of the narrow stairs, a steel ladder with

railings on one side that go way the hell up. They rise slowly, up and up like ants along the staircase. Roslin can't look down. Speakers from the field below send up the voice of Elvis Presley asking "Are You Lonesome To-night?" his long, soft Os drifting up through the dark. Guthrie looks at the people on the ground, running around like insects. And then a young woman's voice far-ther up is saying, "Let me by! Let me pass! 'Scuse me!" and she's wriggling down between the riders.

"She lost her nerve," the guy behind them says when she passes. "But she sure was cute."

Someone on the ground lets a balloon loose, and it sails right up close to the railings. Guthrie leans over to grab it, but it's too far out.

"Don't lean out like that," Roslin says. "It scares the shit out of me."

"This thing's sound as a rock, see?" Guthrie says, and jumps on the step. The whole staircase wobbles like a snake's back.

"Uh-huh. I'm going back down. Right now." She turns and looks down at the line of people jammed in tight be-tween the railings. The incline was gradual, their progress slow, but they're right up there. She shudders and grips the railings, shaky.

Guthrie puts his arm around her. He tries to guess her age, but she's the type where you never know. Forty? Forty-five?

"Don't think about it, honey. Just keep going. You're safe with me." He smiles. He likes this lady from the per-

[81]

sonals, and just think he got her for twenty-five dollars plus lunch. He feels drunk and optimistic all of a sudden.

They can see the man at the top now, timing the admission of people into the chute, pushing their backs with his strong, automatic hand, people disappearing over the edge, screaming.

Chuck Berry comes on the speakers singing "You Never Can Tell."

"That's our song!"

They'd sung it twice on the journey.

"Oooh Baby!"

Guthrie sings, doesn't give a damn who's there listening. Roslin looks at him, thinking about what's to come, about her man at home who's probably sniffing out the kitchen right now looking for his dinner, reading the note she left on the icebox. Guthrie smiles as he sings, belting out the lyrics like he's singing for his supper. That would make a nice change.

The fingertips on her shoulder feel like thimbles from all the work at the mill.

Either they are gonna do this thing or they aren't, and right now Roslin figures they are and he isn't gonna pussy-foot around like some guys. What they want is right there on the surface. She will do this. She will go with this man in the blue shirt to some cheap motel where half the letters on the sign don't light up anymore and hope it's the beginning of something. Jesus. Finally, after ten years, she's getting what she wants, somebody who'll make her feel like she's alive again, like she's somebody under her clothes.

She takes off Guthrie's hat, puts it on her own head, and runs the leather up under her chin. Guthrie laughs and feels the breeze lift what's left of his hair. Roslin points to her head and says, "'Fraid I got tired wearing the hat."

"You're mighty sassy all of a sudden."

They are almost there.

The woman before them is middle-aged. The hand comes out and pushes just as she is hitching up her skirt and then she slides, screaming, down the chute, her hair flying, and it's their turn.

They put their sacks down one on top of the other. He sits down first.

"You two going together?" the hand asks.

"Yeah."

"Well, let the lady up front."

She hooks the strap of her purse across her shoulder and gets in between his knees. His thighs clamp instantly to her sides.

"Hold on!"

She looks down. It is even steeper than she imagined. When it happens, it happens fast. The hand doesn't ask if they're ready, all it does is push.

The Singing Cashier

Smethers, the postman, that greasy fuck with his brown letters. Here he comes in his proud-blue uniform. It's another day, another dense, bright space to blacken in. He strides up the street to our porch, slicks his hair back underneath his cap, and talks in through the letter box.

"Morning, girls!"

The voice is treacle sweet, reaching down the hall as if to grope us. He lives next to a distant cousin of ours who owns a fresh fish van up past the Mormon Road, brings us cod or lemon sole or whiting wrapped in newspaper.

"Yoo-hoo, ladies! Oh, girls!"

The stink of him. The come-and-get-me voice on him. Something's not right. We had fish three times last week, fresh salmon once, and this cousin's someone we hardly know, a woman with a van Mam mentioned.

"Yoo-hoo! Ladies!"

My sister Cora doesn't budge. She leans her elbow on the corner of the gas cooker and pulls on her morning cigarette, exhaling thin little beams of smoke. She never talks until that fag's stubbed out. Behind our kitchen wall, the quick snorts of a knitting machine that wake us up, continue. When our neighbors first moved in, we thought it was him snoring, that their headboard was against our wall, but we were wrong. Here we do not know our next-door neighbors. Mam used to talk about neighbors. People playing poker until all hours, men raising a huge tent together for a marquee on the square, pulling the ropes down tight around the stakes.

Cora takes a last pull, squashes out the butt, and tightens the belt of her lilac dressing gown. I watch her bare footprints fade on the lino as she opens the door and lets him in.

"A vision in the mornings," he says, his eyes starting at her bare feet and traveling up like she's something he would sketch. His lips are shiny with his own spit. "Oh, the versatility of the postal system. The service! Where would you girls be without us?" He hands over the parcel and an electric bill, plops his satchel on the hall stand. A little rub of the hands, a glance around. "Well, Cora, a cup a tea would be sweet."

Rewards for the messenger.

My no-nonsense sister puts up with him. She needs his smelly parcels, I suppose, and cups of tea are cheap enough. She stares into the fridge, inventing breakfast. There's two eggs, a tub of Flora margarine, a wilted head of lettuce, the bright light showing up the emptiness. She shuts the door and plugs the kettle in. It's Wednesday, and we're down to the last few tea bags, so the cups will be peppered with dust today. Smethers sits down snug in the armchair. Cora turns on the radio, tunes into Jimmy Young, who's giving things away. Then she wriggles a coin out of her purse and hands it over.

[85]

"Will you go down and get me a box of matches?"

"Matches? But there's—"

"Piss off now, there's a love."

She gives me the "Just do it" look, so I stomp down to the newsagent's in Breswill Street, a good ten-minute walk each way, but I come home too soon and notice Smethers's belt is notched up tight and Cora's nightdress is inside out, her hands fidgeting with the fuzz around her slipper. And the smell, like sleep gone sticky. Oatmeal boiled over.

Now I'm wise. I take my time. I dawdle to the shops and back, steal a bottle of milk from a blue door's step and sip it all the way into town, small creamy sips that thin down and get sickening towards the bottom. I buy a box of matches or whatever Cora asks for in the shops so we'll never have to talk. Through the jeweler's window I watch ladies trying on rings with big, precious stones, the Scottish assistant coaxing them up over their knuckles and prising them off again.

The wind accumulates in this town, cold gusts trapped by the rows of identical, red brick houses, some built in crescents like they're competing for the sunshine and the air. I stand out here among the preschoolers and the café women sharing their gossip and ashtrays. Other girls my age are in school, wearing scratchy, plaid uniforms and swotting over O levels. I had enough of that, and Cora didn't seem to mind, said it was up to me. I burned my schoolbooks slowly in a barrel out in the yard, pages of algebra, home economics, continents curling up in flame and diminishing to ash. But now sometimes I miss it because there's nothing else to do, nobody my own age, just the afternoon soaps and payday and whatever brain wave Cora thinks up in the days before she gets her period.

Going home, I trail my hands along the railings until the railings disappear and the pavement gets uneven. Sometimes Smethers leaves the gate open and the dogs get in and cock their legs on the hydrangea, but I always wait in the porch and listen, just in case. Our porch is littered with warped plaster slabs, dried-out putty tins, things we never bothered to clear out after Dad.

Cora sings. She comes home from work and says, "They're starting to call me the singing cashier down at Tesco's. They're all saying how nice it is to hear somebody happy."

"Are you?"

"Am I what?" she asks.

"Happy."

"Happy? Happy?" She pats my head, and laughs. "Put the kettle on, ya daft love."

She drinks it black, holds the cup up close to her face and blows out small breaths against the steam. I love her like this. When she sits and thinks up ways to keep us safe from the outside world. Ways to keep this dingy house insulated from the coppers and the gas man, the TV license woman with her sturdy little clipboard.

The photo of our father has fallen off the wall, but his frame leans against the skirting board, determined. It's a picture taken at Pembroke Dock with a trucker's meaty arm around each shoulder. A lorry load of construction men packed up for the crossing and the duty-free. His eyes are dark and feisty. Neither one of us has bothered to replace the nail, to hang that bastard back up in our lives.

Upstairs, Cora showers, getting ready to go out with the other Tesco girls. She sings a song from her new Nina Simone album, her voice high and brittle as a boy's:

> *Take me to the water!*
> *Take me to the water!*
> *Take me to the water to be baptised.*

"Make sure the iron's not too hot!" she shouts down.

In rainy months like these we air our clothes by ironing them. Last time I scorched the backside of her polyester nightdress, leaving a triangular patch of brown. I don't like to think these things might be deliberate.

Outside, in a house opposite ours, lights come on; Japanese lanterns hang like fake moons in the windows. They are pretty shades of blush pink and curd yellow.

And that's the last good night of sleep we had because of what it said in the newspapers. Smethers comes early and uses the bell for once.

"Open up!"

Newspaper but no fish today. His cap is off and I think our distant cousin with the caravan must be dead, but it's worse than that. "Nightmare on Cromwell Street," the headline reads. Cora sucks in breath and lights a Rothman off the gas. Slowly, we take it all in. Two blocks down, the body of a teenage girl has been found under the floor-boards, another buried in the garden. One photo shows Fred and Rosemary West smiling at a Christmas party in the seventies. Another shows them handcuffed, sur-rounded by coppers. There are plans for an excavation.

The very first thought that comes into my mind is milk. That door was blue. I examine the unsuspicious terrace house in the photo, with number 25 hung in trellis on the dash, and then I know it's true: I drank Fred West's milk while my sister was fucking the postman.

My father knew him. Fred West came here, ate supper in our house. A brickie on the river side, his shoes were big and glossy black. A hairy man with a beard and dark eyebrows feeding into one another. Hairy. Like you'd have to blow on him to find out where his eyes are, but the papers show him clean shaven with a reckless look, a savagery made noticeable by truth. I sat up on his lap, and, united, we played against my sister in a game of check-ers. I remember his big fingers clasping the pieces, jump-ing hers, doubling them into kings at the far side of the board and turning back again, taking more.

This morning Cora does not tell me to go out. Instead, I am to put the kettle on. She leads Smethers down the hall, pushes him back against the wall. I hear her voice but not the words, and a few minutes later he's slithering off down the street without a word, moving out of our lives. Finally, he brought something she could not stomach. Those girls were my age. It could have been me. Cora sent me out to

Claire Keegan

run fake errands on what must have been the most dangerous street in England so she could shag a man for the sake of a few parcels. Suddenly I wish Mam was alive. I wish she was alive so Cora wouldn't have to mother me, feed me.

"That's the end of him," she says, gathering up the paper again.

"I was tired of fish anyway. Maybe you'll shag a butcher next."

She doesn't smile. Perhaps she cannot. She just sits under the window with her ankles tucked in under her backside and turns the pages of the newspaper. Behind her the sun is rising, gathering strength over the houses. In the morning light her hair looks dry and broken at the ends. She looks old today, not tired, but less ambitious, like somebody who's quit so she can move on.

I crack two eggs into the frying pan and watch their edges whiten.

"Dad knew him," she says.

"Yeah."

I tip the pan so the oil cooks the whites into a shape. Throw a couple of bread slices into the fat.

"They built that porch together. Jesus."

"Hard or runny?" I ask.

"What?"

"Your egg. Hard or runny?"

"Runny."

She's looking at the photograph of Dad with his trucker friends. For a moment I think she may pick it up, but she doesn't. She looks down, continues to read the newspaper. She has my father's jaw, a squareness to her face I never noticed until now, determination, but her eyes say otherwise. My sister, the singing cashier, looks ready to cry.

"One runny egg," I say, sliding the yellow eye and the fried bread onto a chipped plate, a little border of forget-me-nots growing in a blue snarl around its edge.

"Get that down you," I say. "You'll feel better."

Burns

They will try it out for summer. Together, they will confront their past, the source of all their trouble, and stamp it out. That, at least, is the theory.

On their first night they sit out in front of the house, three children, their father, and Robin, his new wife. The children sit on the porch swing without speaking. The sky is a spooky, policeman blue. The eldest boy, whose legs are longest, pushes them off the railings with his feet, his brother and sister at either side of him. Their father sits in the rocking chair, but he does not rock. Instead, he is remembering smells of lint and ointment, gauze packed in aluminum foil, iced vinegar for a scald. His new wife stands at the railings filing her nails. Physically, she is the exact opposite of the children's mother, a plain, flat-chested woman with dark, waist-length hair. Everyone is listening. Tall pines are grooming the wind (Who's there? it seems to ask: Who? Who?). The chair's chains creak. Down the field something rattles, a cow, scratching herself against a gate perhaps. The children keep swinging, colliding with the darkness. When the girl closes her eyes, her father picks her up and carries her inside. His sons, not wishing to be left alone with their stepmother, soon follow.

The bedroom light comes on, shines out feebly through dirty panes. Robin hears mattresses sinking on springs, sneakers falling on wooden floors, the snap of an elastic waistband, a zipper, low voices. It is dark and starry and there are snakes out there. A graveled road leading to a strange house, the smell of must and cattle, pools of rainwater trapped in the potholed yard.

Her husband comes out and walks the porch. When he speaks, his voice is resonant and tender. She is not sorry she married him.

"Nobody's saying we can't go back, Robin. Nothing's final. You know that."

"I know." She reaches out, squeezes his hand.

"We have to come to terms with this thing. If it doesn't work out, we can always go back to town, no damage done. You understand?"

She nods her head in the gloom.

"Christ, it's like traveling back in time. I keep expecting to hear the cutlery drawer slam. That was the kickoff, she'd whack the drawer of knives shut, and you could smell trouble." He grips the railings until his knuckles turn white. "You see this swing? I got this put up here for the boy, so he'd be able to swing in his bare feet and cool off the scalds. Jesus." He shakes his head, as if everything is beyond him. "I have been such a fool for so long."

"Come to bed, honey," Robin says, taking his hand.

Their belongings, boxes and carryalls, are dumped all over the floors, but she finds her way by the glow of the children's night-light through to the back bedroom. They undress and lie down without bothering to wash or brush their teeth. Robin pulls the blanket up around her chin. In the darkness, she can't make him out. She can't get over how dark it is out here. If somebody paid her a million dollars, she wouldn't walk down that graveled road alone. She rolls into the warmth of her husband's body, feels sleep tugging, pulling her under, and as she is giving in, letting go, she remembers that this is where his ex-wife slept.

In the morning, they prop the doors and windows open, and a fresh wind travels through the house. Some of the window latches are stiff; there are cobwebs in every corner. The boys inspect dead moths and insects on the sills, turn them over with toothpicks, counting their legs, pulling their wings off.

"Gross!" the girl says, finding a baby cockroach under an old Cornflakes box in the pantry.

A thick, white dust hangs over everything. The girl writes her name on the countertop. (She has just recently learned to read and write.) The stuffed stag head above the fireplace looks like he's come in from the snow. Robin hates his plastic, watching eyes, and there's something dreary about the kitchen, with its orange walls, the blue, wooden geese flying in a V above the sink, the wobbly kitchen table.

They breakfast on junk food, leftovers from the journey: crackers, cheese, tortilla chips. Robin digs some instant coffee from a jar, boils water in a pot. Much of the cutlery in the drawers is rusted. When she opens the refrigerator, she sees pickles floating in a jar of green vinegar, dried-out garlic bulbs, shriveled hot dogs.

"Who's for a shot of penicillin?" she asks, holding up a moldy tomato.

After breakfast they explore the house. The living area is all on the second floor: the country kitchen, a big, high-ceilinged living room, three bedrooms with baths, and a dormitory with eight single beds. (The extended family used to come up for Thanksgivings.) Off the kitchen, a junk room with a washing machine and dryer, a cradle, a wall of shelves stacked tight with paint cans, toddlers' toys, Frisbees, charcoal. Everything faded from too much sun. They descend the steps from the living room down to the ground floor, which is empty. Nothing down there, only a musty feeling, a concrete floor, old smells of leather, roots, and mice. The middle boy stands at the top of the steps and watches them descend and return, but he does not venture down.

The yard stretches down to a black barn with stalls, hay bales, a chicken shed with toadstools inside the door. At the far side of the house, trees are sprouting small, hard peaches. The morning sun throws this side of the house into deep and palpable shadow. Bamboo canes for supporting peas and beans still stand askew in the vegetable patch. The boys dislodge them from the earth and throw them like javelins across the tall weeds. The girl is quiet, carrying her stuffed giraffe, holding him up to peep in through the cracks in the chicken shed, the stalls in the barn, reading the brand names on empty feed bags.

When the boys ride into town with their father for supplies, Robin takes the girl down the field to pick wildflowers. The boundaries are blood red with some shrub she cannot name. The girl points out the poison ivy, tells Robin to "watch out," and reaches up to pluck the reddest, heaviest blooms. Robin sees the circular scar on the girl's wrist but says nothing. They walk back through swishing, buttercupped grasses to the house. The girl finds old cans from plum tomatoes in the junk room, peels their faded labels off, revealing shiny, silver tin underneath, and arranges the red flowers while Robin sweeps the floors.

"Have you ever seen such dust?" says Robin.

The girl laughs, and the boys come back with brown paper bags of groceries and McDonald's Happy Meals. Their father has brought drinking water for the fountain. When the girl climbs onto a stool, the table wobbles and her drink spills. A look of terror passes over the face. She begins to cry out of all proportion.

"Hey!" says her father. "Hey, my baby girl, what's wrong? Here, it doesn't matter. Here, have mine."

He sits her on his lap and gives her a sip out of his drink, dips a french fry into ketchup and tells her she is a good girl, his girl, to eat up, that soon she will be as tall as those weeds in the yard, but the girl slides down between his knees and crouches under the shelter of the table.

That night in bed, after the children have gone to sleep and doors are locked, they talk.

"Maybe I'm just opening a can of worms, coming up here," he says. "Taking the kids up here. Opening a big can of worms."

"I don't think so, honey."

"It's like the bitch is still here. I feel it. The children feel it," he says. "Did you see her today, just spilling her drink, how upset she was? Maybe this just isn't necessary. All that psychobabble bullshit about confronting the past." He reaches out to turn the fan up a notch. He feels hot in these rooms, too hot for comfort, even though it's autumn. "We were in a restaurant one time, and she spilled her grape juice. Well, you know grape juice, the way it stains. It was a fancy place, too, a white tablecloth and all. Well, my wife lost her rag, reached out and whacked our little girl across the face before I could move."

"Jesus."

He sips water from a plastic cup. Some of the hairs on his belly have turned white.

"Maybe we should do the place up different, make it over, change things around," Robin says. "We could ask some of the kids' friends up. It's not like there isn't room."

"Maybe." He wipes his forehead. "Maybe we should shake holy water around, get the preacher in. Maybe we should set a match to this place and hightail it out of here. Go back home, get our heads examined."

"Don't worry," she says, scratching his hair. "Everything'll be okay, you'll see."

"I hope so," he says, punching up the pillows. "I certainly hope so."

Claire Keegan

* * *

The first thing they tackle is the kitchen. They move out all the furniture, the dresser, the wobbly table, take the wooden ducks and the fire extinguisher off the walls, and empty out the cabinets. They draw a design for a new kitchen on the back of an old Whitney Bank calendar. An island is what they decide on. Something they can all sit around and cook at. They let each child choose a name from "Carpenters" in the yellow pages and call for estimates.

When the week's over, their island is built in the center of the kitchen. Nothing fancy, just a tall rectangular counter with cabinets underneath. The gas man has piped in a supply for a hob. Robin takes the girl down to the co-op, and they choose pretty, brick-red tiles for the countertops, decorative tiles with beige leaves for the border. Together they mix grout in a basin and lay it all down. She lets the girl stay up late to help her while everybody else is sleeping. She buys six director's chairs, the kind where you can take the canvas seats off and throw them in the washing machine, gets an electrician to install dimmer switches above the hob. The boys screw crooks into the beam overhead and hang all the cooking utensils from the ceiling.

The night it's finished, their father drives down to the Winn-Dixie market for root beer. Robin has a tray of lasagna in the oven, and she's baking a chocolate cake for dessert. The kids kneel on the director's chairs around the island and help out. Robin puts the eldest boy in charge of sifting the flour and cocoa while she beats the butter and sugar with a wooden spoon. The girl measures out the teaspoons of baking powder and cornstarch and greases the tin with butter while her brother whisks the eggs. Robin gives everyone a turn at the mixing bowl, smiles at the eldest boy, who is left-handed and mixes counterclockwise. She checks the oven, pours the batter in the tin. The children lick the bowl clean.

"Okay," says Robin, "your dad'll be home soon. Let's clear up."

Robin lights a candle and places it on the middle of the island, dims the lights. She reaches out for the red flowers on the sill and notices something at her feet. At first she thinks it's a mouse. She is not afraid of mice. The girl is the first to scream. The children instinctively climb up on the island for safety and knock the lighted candle over.

And that is how their father finds them: his three children and his new wife screaming, a naked flame, a fire starting in the kitchen, and the floor moving. He douses the candle quickly before it catches and looks down at the floor. He has never seen anything like it. For some reason, he cannot move. Instead, he remembers an old black-and-white movie with locusts descending on a field somewhere in Africa, wiping out an entire crop, a livelihood, in minutes.

Cockroaches are everywhere. Hard-bodied, shiny roaches. They are crawling around the island, scuttling up the cabinet doors, behind the taps, underneath the water fountain. They swirl in behind the red flowers that smell like cat piss on the sill. The sound they make is not unlike the sound of drizzling rain. The children are standing on the island. The eldest boy reaches for the cooking utensils on the beam, the serving spoon, the fish-slice, the ladle, and hands them to his siblings. They start killing. They stamp on them with their sneakers. The girl, reluctant at first, rolls her sleeves up, to get a good whack at them. Robin runs into the junk room. Her shoes make an awful sound with every step. She brings out tennis racquets and a plastic baseball bat, and she too starts killing. Her husband is mesmerized. His new wife is killing with both hands.

"Don't just stand there!" she screams. "Help us!"

She hands him the baseball bat, opens a cabinet door under the island, and a fresh invasion spills out on the floor. A darting stream is crawling up from what seems to be the heart of the house, from downstairs into the center of the kitchen. A surge of children's voices, piercing and irreverent, thunders through the house. Everyone clambers, is covetous to kill them.

"Come on!" The father is shouting. "Come on, you bitches!"

They cannot say how long it is before the shiny stream of roaches dwindles to a trickle and stops. The father's eyebrows are wet with sweat, the elastic in the girl's ponytail has fallen within an inch of her hair's end, the boys are breathing as they would after a football game. They do not smell their dinner, burning. They are watching. They are listening. Every one, listening. They can hear their own heartbeats. When a drop of water falls, plop, into the sink, they move violently, as one.

Quare Name for a Boy

I have come home to tell you. I have walked back into my past, my clothes too small for me, a story from a women's magazine.

I've come back before, bought ferry crossings for engagement parties, my nephew's christening, and that Christmas when I met you. You chatted me up over the hors d'oeuvres, fed me pâté on melba toast as we stood between a besequined hostess and a man in black. I was your Christmas fling, a thing to break the boredom of the holidays, and you were mine. But now these suitcases have the weight of anchors on this floor I learned to walk on. It may be I'm back for good, but nothing is certain.

My female relatives huddle around me in the bedroom, have brought up tea, china cups and saucers excavated from the sideboard, the clink of crockery on trays. They're tweedy, big-boned women who like to think they taught me right from wrong, manners, and the merits of hard work. They are flat-bellied, temperamental women who've given up and call it happiness. We come from women who comfort men, men who never say no. Now they fill their best teacups, asking about my future, asking, "What is it you do now?" and "What are you going to do now?" which isn't quite the same thing.

[101]

"I'm going to write," I say. A smutty novel, I want to add, something lecherous and bawdy, make *Fanny Hill* look like your Sunday missals. The answer to the question is I don't know.

Writing is a queer occupation, especially at my age. They calculate my age, trying to remember what happened around the time I was born, who died. They're not too sure, but I'm no spring chicken anymore. I should be doing something else by now, latching myself onto some unmarried man with a steady wage and a decent car.

"You and your books," they say, shaking their heads, squeezing the good out of the tea bags.

They don't know the half of it, don't know the disguises I've made for them, how I took twenty years off their hard-earned faces, washed the honey-blond rinses out of their hair, how I put them in another country and changed their names. I have turned these women inside out like dirty old socks. The lies I've told.

I unpack my suitcases, and the ritual begins. They lean in from the bed, the armchair, the window seat, and make conversation, wondering about my clothes, if my shoes are patent, my dresses silk. I am like an American cousin. They finger the fabric, see how deep the hems are, read the labels, ruminate:

"Nice bit a stuff in that, where'd ya come at it?"

"Be the flip, look at the miniskirt!"

"But sure the minis are all in again, don't you know?"

"She has the legs."

"Lovely bit of linen in that, but the devil wouldn't iron it."

"Can't beat the drip-dry, really, can ya?"

"What size is that? Would that fit me?"

"You've put on a bit of weight if ya don't mind me saying so. But you have the height, you can carry it."

I drape practical cotton blouses, flared elasticized skirts across wire hangers, a black wool trouser suit, a jogging suit. Practical shoes that belie my occupation. A pair of red high heels to confuse them. They rummage through my things, trying to find out who I am.

Eventually, they retreat into the kitchen to prepare dinner. It's getting on for five; the men will soon be home. I hear the clunk of potatoes in the sink, the clatter of saucepan lids, and soon the smell of boiled turnip drifts upstairs.

I had forgotten how these back rooms bruised yellow in the evenings. I sit under the window and read with my face in the shade and my book in the sunlight and wonder if it's bad for my eyes, crossing that distance. I read *Jamaica Inn*, the first book that lured me into this deception and think Daphne would be a good name if it's a girl.

I have arranged to meet you in Dublin. You look handsome and tall in your cowboy boots. You kiss my neck in greeting, but your lips are cold. And something I do not remember, a gold stud, shines in your left earlobe. You tell me the English air must suit me, that I'm blooming.

"You're looking well, whatever you're doing with yerself across the water," you say with something that sounds like disapproval.

Irish girls should dislike England, they should stay on their own turf and raise their sons up right, stuff the chicken, snip the parsley, tolerate the blare of the Sunday game.

"I'm a hooker, did you not know?"

"Well, your tongue's not changed." You laugh and loop your arm through mine and take me out to Sandycove, the granite dome of Joyce's tower mushrooming into the cold afternoon sun.

"He wrote all them famous books. Imagine," you say. "And this is the snot-green sea."

A ruffle of dirty sea splashes against the rocks overlooking Gentleman's Beach. A naked, middle-aged man comes out of the water. I lie down and pull my coat up around me. The salt wind is sharp, would cut the arse off a girl. We stay there for a long time without saying a word, our thoughts forking out separately.

I remember the story of a young woman someplace down west. They found her in a hut her father'd built, a one-roomed cabin without a chimney. In a wood, he'd kept her and let her die sooner than let a neighbor know she was having a child. I can still see the photos: a stretcher with a body bag, another of her smiling in a school group, her head and shoulders circled.

A boat passes with men's voices singing, "My! My! My! Deeelilah!" We watch them go into deeper water, towards Howth.

You think it's funny.

"Idiots," you say, smiling.

You have always liked other men's pleasure, taking a small share of it for yourself. I would have thought it was funny too, if I didn't know what I know now. I used to think I could never know too much. In college, I couldn't get enough. I stacked the books up high on the bedside locker, read late into the night, and traded them in for more, as if learning was something I could reduce over time. But now I know too much; like an eavesdropper I feel I have overheard an irrefutable story about myself, and so I must go slowly, must keep this to myself until I'm ready. Like holding a full glass, not being able to move, afeared of spills.

Rain comes down along the headland, I see the gentle, gray sweep of it moving indiscriminately south. The gulls swoop down and shit on the rocks, staying ahead of the weather. I sense this is the last time we will ever be like this. Everything casual between us will end here.

"Let's shag off for a drink."

We walk away from the sea's edge, towards the town. The pub is dark and warm, with brown, sepia photographs of hurling teams hanging on the walls, the men in the front row genuflecting for the camera. You check the bar, and I remember a gang of cronies you talked about but never introduced me to. Three middle-aged men sit at the counter with their *Evening Herald*s, circling the hot fillies, taking a chance on the dogs, talking odds. You carry two pints to a table like a man carrying the first two bucketfuls of water to put out a blaze in his own stable. Hurried, ready to go again.

We sit in red armchairs by the fire, and those nights come back to me, that week between Christmas and the new year, six days and nights spent at your mother's empty house, when I wore nothing but your clothes, your mandarin-collared shirts that came down to my knees, your thick, brown-heeled football socks. We stayed in and ate takeouts: chow mein, fresh cod and chips, beef Korma, the strangest Christmas food. I remember the Japanese flag hanging in the corner of the room, the center dipped in red like a truce gone bloody. The way you took it down and snapped it out, let it fall down over my naked body in your mother's king-size bed. Maybe I should have known.

We used to wake in the middle of the night to make love and coffee, and you didn't have much to say but that was fine. I sat up and listened to the cars passing through the slush, the odd drunk bar of "Silent Night" from the merry stragglers going home. The drizzle on the glass blistering the view of Georgian houses.

And now I wonder what it is you expect. Another six-day fling? I suspect you think I'm a woman who doesn't have the tact to let go of a small thing like a week in your mother's bed.

"Has the cat got yer tongue?" you ask.

And then all my preparations disappear. The words come out blunt and fast and irreversible. That is always the attraction to writing; with writing it's possible to change the words, to get a second chance.

Your hand tightens around your glass. I wait for you to say something. I want you to say you love me, even though I don't love you. It might restore the balance. If I must carry the child, the least you can do is love me.

Green wood hisses in the grate, the resin oozing out from under the bark. Lines of connecting sparks, what my grandmother called soldiers, march across the soot. She said that was a sign of bad weather, but you say nothing. Whatever you say, I'll manage. I will live out of a water barrel and check the skies. I will learn fifteen types of wind and know the weight of tomorrow's rain by the rustle in the sycamores. Make nettle soup and dandelion bread, ask for nothing. And I won't comfort you. I will not be the woman who shelters her man same as he's a boy. That part of my people ends with me.

You watch the fellows at the bar, young men in their early twenties with leather jackets, blue jeans, free men. You could get up and walk over there in seven or eight cowboy strides. You drink your stout until the froth settles halfway down the glass. I watch your Adam's apple moving like a stone in your throat.

"Well, the damage is done now," you say.

I reach across the table and wipe the froth from your upper lip, but touching brings the memory of touch, and you pull away.

"What do you think of the name Daphne?"

And there it is, my decision named. No boat trip, no roll of twenty-pound notes, no bleachy white waiting room with dog-eared women's magazines at the clinic.

You peer into your glass.

"It's a quare name for a boy," you say.

You push those cold lips into a smile. Your expression is not unlike that of the hurlers in the photograph, and I suspect pride. Because pride is something I know about. I won't keep you away from the boys and your smoky, poolroom nights. I'll drink this parting glass, but at the end of the evening I'll shake your hand. I'll be damned if I'll snare you like a fox, live with you that way, look into your eyes some night years from now and discover a man whose worst regret is six furtive nights spent in his mother's bed with a woman from a Christmas party. Suddenly, I wonder why I came.

"Drink up," you say, gesturing to my glass. "A girl in your condition needs lots of iron."

"Cheers."

"Cheers."

Our glasses touch. I drink my stout, taking comfort in the fact that there are minerals hidden in the white stripe of its head.

Sisters

It is customary for the Porters to send a postcard to say when they will be arriving. Betty waits. Each time the dog barks she finds herself going to the window at the foot of the stairs, looking out through the maidenhair fern to see if the postman is cycling up the avenue. It is almost June. The chill has slackened off; plums are getting plumper on the trees. The Porters will soon come, demanding strange foods, fresh handkerchiefs, hot water bottles, ice.

Louisa, Betty's sister, went away to England when she was young and married Stanley Porter, a salesman who fell for her, he said, because of the way her hair fell down her back. Louisa always had beautiful hair. When they were young, Betty brushed it every night, one hundred strokes, and secured the gold braid with a piece of satin ribbon.

Betty's own hair is, and always has been, an unremarkable brown. Her hands were always her best feature, white, ladylike hands that played the organ on Sundays. Now, after years of labor, her hands are ruined, the skin on her palms hard and masculine, the knuckles enlarged; she has put washing-up liquid and castor oil on her fingers, but her mother's wedding band cannot be removed.

Betty lives in the homestead, the big house, as it is called. It once belonged to a Protestant landlord who sold up and moved away after a childless marriage ended. The Land Commission, which bought the estate, knocked down the three-story section of the house and sold the remaining two-story servants' quarters and the surrounding seventy acres to Betty's father for a small sum when he married. The house looks too small for the garden and too close to the yard, but its ivy-covered walls look handsome nonetheless. The archway leads to a yard with stables, a barn and granite sheds, a coach house, kennels, and the well. There's a fine, walled orchard at the back, where in the old days the landlord grazed an Angus bull to keep the children out, seeing as he had none of his own. The place has a history, a past. People said Parnell had a tooth pulled in the parlor. The big kitchen has a barred window, an Aga stove and the oak table Betty scrubs on Saturdays. The white, marble fireplace in the parlor suits the mahogany furniture. A staircase curves on to a well-lighted landing with oak doors opening into three large bedrooms overlooking the yard, and a bathroom Betty had installed when her father became ill.

Betty, too, had wanted to go to England, but she stayed back to keep the house. Their mother died suddenly when Betty and Louisa were small. She went out to gather wood one afternoon and dropped dead coming back through the meadow. It seemed natural for Betty, being the eldest, to step into her mother's shoes and mind her father, a humorsome man given to violent fits of temper. She hadn't an easy life. There were cattle to be herded and tested, pigs to fatten, turkeys to be sent off on the train to Dublin before Christmas. They cut the meadow in summer and harvested fields of barley and oats in autumn.

Her father gave instructions and did less and less, paid a man to come in and do the hardest work. He criticized the veterinary bills, insulted the priest who came to anoint him when he was ill, belittled Betty's cooking, and claimed that nothing was as it should have been. Nothing was the way it used to be, he meant. He hated change. Toward the end, he'd put on his black overcoat and walk the fields, seeing how tall the grass was in the meadow, counting the grains of corn on the stalks, noting the thinness of a cow or the rust on a gate. Then he would come inside just before dark and say, "Not much time left. Not much time."

"Don't be morbid," Betty used to answer, and continued on; but last winter her father took to his bed, and for the three days preceding his death he lay there roaring and kicking his feet, calling for "Buttermilk! Buttermilk!"

When he died on a Tuesday night, by willing himself to die, Betty was more relieved than sorry.

Betty kept track of Louisa's progress through the years; her wedding, which she did not attend, the birth of her children, one boy and one girl, what Louisa had wanted. She sent a fruit cake through the post every Christmas, homemade fudge at Easter, and remembered the children's birthdays, put pound notes she could not spare in cards.

Betty had never married. She had once walked out with a young Protestant man named Cyril Dawe her father disapproved of. Nothing ever came of it. The time for marriage and children passed for Betty. She became used to attending to her father's needs in the big house, quelling his temper, making his strong tea, ironing his shirts, and polishing his good shoes on a Saturday night.

After his death she managed to live by renting out the land and carefully spending the savings her father had left in the Allied Irish Bank. She was fifty years old. The house was hers, but a clause in her father's will gave Louisa right of residence for the duration of her life. Her father had always favored Louisa. She had given him admiration, whereas Betty only fed and clothed and cared for him.

When June passes without word from the Porters, Betty becomes uneasy. She pictures the lettuce and the scallions rotting in the vegetable patch, toys with the notion of renting a guest house by the sea, of going off to Ballymoney or Cahore Point; but in her heart she knows she won't. She never goes anywhere. All she ever does is cook and clean and milk the cow she keeps for the house, attend mass on Sundays. But she likes it this way, likes having the house to herself, knowing things are as she left them.

An overwhelming sense of freedom has accompanied the days since her father's death. She pulls weeds, keeps the garden tidy, goes out with the pruners on Saturdays to cut flowers for the altar. She does the things she never had time to do before: she crochets, blues the lace curtains, replaces the bulb in the sacred heart lamp, scrapes the moss off the horse trough, and paints the archway gate. She can make jam later on when the fruit ripens. She can pit the potatoes and pickle the tomatoes in the greenhouse.

Nothing, really, will go to waste if the Porters do not come. She is getting used to this idea of living through the summer alone, is humming a tune softly and weighing candied peel on the scales, when the postman wheels the bicycle up to the door.

"They're coming on the ninth off the evening ferry, Miss Elizabeth," he says. "They're coming as far as Enniscorthy on the bus. You'll have to send a car." He puts the card on the dresser and slides the kettle over on the hot plate to make himself some tea. "Not a bad day."

Betty nods. She has only four days to get the house ready. They could have given her more notice. It seems strange, their not bringing the car, Stanley's big company car in which he always takes such pride.

The next morning she throws out her father's old vests she's used as dusters, carries the empty stout bottles up the wood and dumps them under the bushes. She takes out rugs and beats them with more vigor than is necessary, raises a flurry of dust. She hides old blankets at the back of the wardrobe, turns the mattresses, and puts the good sheets on the beds. She always keeps good bed linen in case she'll get sick and she wouldn't want the doctor or the priest saying her sheets are patched. She takes all the cracked and chipped plates off the dresser and arranges the good willow-pattern dinner set on the shelves. She orders bags of flour and sugar and wheaten meal from the grocer, gets down on her knees and polishes the floor until it shines, scrubs the toilet and the bath, buys a new hinge for the dresser door, and gets her hair set.

They arrive on a hot Friday evening. Betty takes off her apron when the taxi beeps the horn and rushes out to greet them.

"Oh Betty!" Louisa says, as if she's surprised to see her there.

Louisa looks young as ever in her white summer two-piece, her hair hanging in gold waves down her back. Her bare arms are brown with the sun.

Her son, Edward, has grown tall and lanky, a sullen young man who prefers to stay indoors; he extends a cold palm, which Betty shakes. There is little feeling in his handshake. The girl, Ruth, skips down to the old tennis court without so much as a word of hello.

"Come back here and kiss your aunt Betty!" Louisa screams.

"Where's Stanley?"

"Oh he's busy, had to work, you know," Louisa says. "He may follow on later."

"Well, you're looking great, as usual."

Louisa accepts but does not return the compliment. Her white teeth are too plentiful for her smile. The taxi man is taking suitcases off the roof rack. There is an awful lot of luggage. They've brought a black Labrador and books and pillows and Wellingtons, a flute, raincoats, a chessboard, and woolly sweaters.

"We brought cheese," Louisa says, and hands Betty a slab of pungent cheddar.

"How thoughtful," Betty says, and sniffs it.

Louisa stands at the front gates and gazes out toward Mount Leinster with its ever lighted mast and the lush deciduous forest in the valley.

"Oh, Betty," she says, "it's so lovely to be home."

"Come on in."

Betty has the table set; two kettles stand boiling on the stove, their spouts expelling pouty little breaths of steam. A pool of evening sunlight falls through the barred window over the cold roast chickens and potato salad.

"Poor Coventry was put in a cage for the entire journey," Louisa says, referring to the dog. He has slumped down in front of the dresser, and Betty has to slide him across the linoleum to open the cupboard doors.

"Any beetroot, Aunt Elizabeth?" Edward asks.

Betty has taken great care washing the lettuce but now finds herself hoping an insect won't crawl out of the salad bowl. Her eyesight isn't what it used to be. She scalds the teapot and cuts a loaf of brown bread into thin, dainty slices.

"I need the toilet!" Ruth announces.

"Take your elbows off the table," Louisa instructs, and removes a hair from the butter dish.

There is too much pepper in the salad dressing, and the rhubarb tart could have used more sugar, but all that's left is a few potato skins, chicken bones, greasy dishes.

When evening falls, Louisa says she'd like to sleep with Betty.

"It'll be like old times," she says. "You can brush my hair."

She has developed an English accent, which Betty doesn't care for. Betty does not want Louisa in her bed. She likes being sprawled out on her double mattress, waking and sleeping when she feels like it, but she can't say no. She puts Edward in her father's room and Ruth in the other and helps Louisa drag her luggage up the stairs.

Louisa pours two measures of duty-free vodka into glasses and talks about the improvements she has made to her house in England. She describes the satin floor-length curtains in the living room, which cost £25 a yard, the velvet headboards, the dishwasher that sterilizes the dishes, and the tumble dryer that means she doesn't have to race out to the line every time a drop of rain falls.

"No wonder Stanley's working," Betty says, and sips the vodka. She doesn't care for the taste; it reminds her of the holy water she drank as a child, thinking it would cure her stomachaches.

"Don't you miss Daddy?" Louisa says suddenly. "He always had such a warm welcome for us."

Betty gives her a straight look, feels the ache in her arms after the four days' work.

"Oh. I don't mean you—"

"I know what you mean," Betty says. "No, I don't really miss him. He was so contrary towards the end. Going out to the fields and talking about death. But then, you brought out the sweeter side of him."

Her father used to hold Louisa in a tight embrace when she arrived home, then stood back to look at her. He used

[116]

to tell Betty to keep fig rolls in the house because she had a taste for figs. Nothing was ever too good for Louisa.

Now she unpacks her clothes, holding them up for Betty to admire. There's a linen dress with pink butterflies swooping toward the tail, a glittery scarf, a burgundy lace slip, a cashmere jacket, leather peep-toe shoes. She takes the lid off a bottle of American perfume and holds it out for Betty to sniff, but she does not spray a sample on her wrist. Louisa's clothes have the luxurious feel of money. The hems are deep, the linings silk; her shoes have leather insoles. She takes a covetous pride in her belongings, but then Louisa has always been the fashionable one.

Before she went to England Louisa got a job house-keeping for a rich woman in Killiney. Once, Betty took the train to Dublin to spend a day with her. When Louisa saw her at the station with her country suit and her brown handbag, she whipped the handbag from her hands, fast as greased lightning, said, "Where do you think you're going with that old thing?" and pushed it down in her shopping bag.

Now she sits at the dressing table singing an old Latin hymn while Betty brushes her hair. Betty listens to her girlish voice and, catching a glimpse of their reflection in the mirror, realizes that nobody would ever suspect they were sisters. Louisa with her gold hair and emerald ear-rings, looking so much younger than her years; Betty with her brown hair and her man's hands and the age showing so plainly on her face.

"Chalk and cheese" was the phrase their mother used.

* * *

Edward wants a poached egg for breakfast. He sits at the head of the table and waits for it to be put in front of him. Betty stands at the stove stirring porridge while Louisa, still in her nightdress, looks into the cupboards, inspecting their contents, seeing what there is to eat.

"I'm starving!" Ruth says. She's plump for a girl of her age.

None of them does anything simply or quietly; they don't mind taking up space, asking for more of this or that. On those rare occasions when Betty goes into anyone's house, she is thankful for what she gets and washes the dishes afterward; but the Porters act like they own the place.

Louisa makes cheese on toast for Ruth but eats little herself. She just pushes her eggs around her plate with a fork and sips her tea.

"You're miles away," Betty says.

"Just thinking."

Betty does not press her: Louisa has always been secretive. When she was beaten in school, she never said one word at home. When falsely blamed for laughing or talking out of turn, Louisa would blankly kneel in front of the picture of Saint Anthony and confess and take undue punishment without ever a mention. Once, after the headmaster hit Betty, her nose would not stop bleeding and he sent her out to the stream to wash her face, but she ran home across the fields and told her mother, who walked her back up to the school, into the classroom, and told the headmaster that if he laid so much as another finger on her girls, he'd get a worse death than Billy the butter maker (who had been savagely murdered down south a few days back). Louisa had jeered her about that, but Betty was unashamed. She would rather tell the truth and face the consequences than get down on her knees before a picture of a saint and confess to things she did not do.

On Sunday morning, Louisa balances their father's old shaving mirror on the crucifix in Betty's window and plucks her eyebrows into perfect semicircles. Betty milks the cow and digs potatoes and gets ready for mass.

A great fuss is made over Louisa in the chapel. Neighbors come up to her in the graveyard and shake her hand, and say she's looking wonderful.

"Aren't you looking great?"

"You haven't aged one bit."

"Sure weren't you always the apple of everybody's eye?"

"Doesn't she look great, Betty?"

When they go into the grocer's for messages, Joe Costello, the bachelor who owns the quarry and rents out Betty's land, corners Louisa between the tinned goods and the cold meats counter.

"Are ya still fond of the cinema?" he asks.

He's a great big man with a pinstripe suit and a black pencil mustache. They used to cycle to the pictures together before Louisa went off to England. Edward is setting mousetraps in the hardware shelves, and Ruth's ice-cream cone is dripping down the front of her dress, but Louisa takes no notice.

"Where's the hubby?" Joe Costello is asking Louisa.

"Oh, he had to work."

"Ah yes, I know the feeling. The work never ends."

When they get home, Betty ties her apron around her waist and puts the dinner on. She likes Sundays, listening to the curate read the gospel, meeting the neighbors, listening to the spit of the roast while she reads the paper, tending the garden in the afternoon, and taking a walk around the wood. She always tries to keep it a day of rest, keep it holy.

"Don't you get lonely up here on your own?" Louisa asks.

"No." It had never occurred to her to be lonely.

Louisa paces the kitchen floor until dinnertime, then takes off down the avenue to visit the neighbors' houses. Betty stays at home and works out a menu for the week. Louisa hasn't given her a penny toward their keep, hasn't bought so much as a loaf. Betty's budget is tight enough without feeding three extra people, but she assumes it's something Louisa will put right when it comes into her mind. Louisa has always been forgetful about the essentials.

Monday is washing day. The Porters don't believe in wearing the same clothes twice, and since Ruth wets the bed, she needs clean sheets every day. Betty wonders at the child—she's almost nine years old—but says nothing to Louisa, sensing it would be a sore point. The clothesline between the lime trees is laden, but a strong wind throws the laundry into a horizontal flapping state that Betty finds pleasurable. Some of the clothes are delicate, and Betty must wash them by hand. As she dips her hands down into the sinkful of soapy water, she begins to wonder when Stanley will arrive. He would take them off to the seaside and skim pebbles across the waves, go fishing for pike in the Slaney, shoot rabbits. Keep the children occupied.

Betty rises earlier to have more time to herself. The summer mornings feel healthy and cool. She sits with her head leaned against the warmth of the cow's side and watches milk dancing in the bucket. She feeds the geese and pulls carrots and parsnips from the vegetable patch. Mount Leinster looks gratifyingly unchanged in the blue distance; swallows are living under the eaves of the granite stables. This is the life she wants to lead, the good life.

She is pouring warm milk through a piece of muslin when Joe Costello blocks the daylight in the doorway.

"Morning, Betty." He tips his hat respectfully.

"Good morning, Joe!" She's surprised to see him, he so seldom drops in, except when a bullock goes missing or to pay the rent on the land.

"Sit down, won't you?"

He sits in at the table, all arms and legs. "Nice spell of weather we're having."

"Couldn't ask for nicer."

She makes tea and sits talking to Joe at the table. He's a decent sort of man, Betty thinks, the way he takes his hat off and uses the spoon for the jam instead of pushing his knife down into the pot. Table manners can reveal an awful lot. They talk about cattle and the quarry, and then Edward appears, pokes his nose into the implements on the sink.

"Isn't the milk here pasteurized, Aunt Betty?"

Betty laughs with Joe Costello over the good of it, but when Louisa comes down, Joe loses all interest in Betty. Louisa isn't wearing her nightdress. Her hair is brushed, and she's in her linen butterfly dress, her mouth shiny with lip gloss.

"Ah, Joe!" she says, as if she didn't know he was there.

"Morning, Louisa." He stands up.

Betty takes it all in, how Louisa flirts: the pout of her lips, the tilt of her hip, the way she lifts and relaxes her bare shoulder. It is a fine art. She leaves them there talking in the kitchen and strides out to the garden looking for parsley. Ruth is standing under the tree, eating her plums.

"Get away from those plums!"

"Okay, okay," Ruth says. "Don't get your knickers in a knot."

"They're for jam, you greedy little girl."

It is an old story. The men flocking around Louisa, sniffing her out. Louisa and Betty went to house dances together when they were young. Betty remembers a fine summer's night, sitting on a wooden bench in Davis's, just a mile up the road. She was sitting there feeling the grain of the wood under her fingers. The scent of lilacs from the ditch came through the open window. She remembers the happiness of that moment being broken when Louisa leaned over. She can still, to this day, remember her exact words:

"I'll give you a piece of advice. You should try not to smile. You look terrible when you smile."

Betty didn't smile for years afterward without remembering that remark. She never had Louisa's white smile. She'd suffered from bronchitis as a child and had to take cough medicine, which ruined her teeth. So many things, all coming back. Betty feels her blood racing, but that is all in the past. She can think for herself now. She has earned that right. Her father is dead. She can see things as they are, not through his eyes, nor Louisa's.

When she comes back into the kitchen with sprigs of parsley, Joe Costello is pouring tea into her best china cup for Louisa.

"Say when."

"When," Louisa says. She is sitting with her back to the harsh morning light, the sun intensifying the gold of her hair.

Betty cooks a leg of lamb the following Sunday. When a trickle of blood runs out on the serving plate while she is carving, she doesn't care. Nor does she care that the carrots are rubbery and overcooked, but nobody makes any mention of the meal, not one word. She's in no mood to cater for individual tastes. Earlier she had gone down into the parlor and caught Ruth jumping on the sofa. What's more, there are dog hairs all over the house. Everywhere she looks there are dog hairs.

Edward hangs around, silently entering the rooms in which she's working and startles her. He cannot entertain himself.

"There's nothing to do," he complains. "We're stranded."

"You can clean out the hen house if you like," Betty says. "The sprong's in the barn."

But somehow this does not appeal to Edward. He's not a fellow who believes in earning his appetite. Ruth sings funny little songs and skips around the garden. Betty feels sorry for her sometimes: Louisa pays her little or no attention, and she's only nine. So when Betty is finished washing the dishes, she reads her "Hansel and Gretel."

"Why would the father desert his own children?" Ruth asks.

"It was a mistake," says Betty. "Everybody's entitled to a few mistakes."

Betty makes jam, takes the stepladder outside, reaches up into the boughs and plucks every single plum off the tree. She washes and stones them, covers the fruit with sugar in the preserving pan, and shows Ruth and Edward how to wash jam jars. They haven't a clue about domestic work. Edward squirts a cupful of Fairy Liquid into the sink, and they have to start again.

"Who does the washing up at home?" Betty asks. "Oh, that's right: you have a dishwasher, I forgot."

"A dishwasher? No, we don't, Aunt Betty," Ruth says.

They make the jam, and Betty lines up the pots like ammunition in the pantry. She's wondering how long it will last, when Louisa walks into the kitchen after her day out visiting. Her expression is flushed and radiant like someone who's been swimming in deep salt waters.

"Any mail?" she asks.

"No."

"Nothing?"

"Just an electric bill."

"Oh."

July has passed without a word from Stanley.

In August the weather turns stormy. Rain keeps the Porters indoors, traps them in the rooms. Wet leaves cling to the windowpanes; black rainwater runs down between the drills in the vegetable patch. Louisa stays in bed reading romantic novels and eating cake, walks around in her nightdress till well past noon. She washes her hair with rainwater and makes Rice Krispies buns for the children. Edward plays the flute in the parlor; Betty has never heard anything like it—it's as if somebody has trapped a wild bird or a small reptile in a cage, and its despairing little voice is crying out to be freed. Ruth cuts pictures of models and perfume out of magazines with Betty's good dressmaking scissors and pastes them in her scrapbook.

Betty becomes concerned about the garden. Strong winds have shaken the rose bushes, scattered the blooms across the gravel, and Betty, picking them up, feels sorry and pets their dusky pink petals, smooth as eyelids in her fingers. There are aphids on the leaves; they are spotted and drowsy. She has been too busy with domestic chores to tend her garden.

She is standing there, thinking about her poor flowers, when Edward approaches her. Elderberry blossoms are being cast about like confetti in the wind; a light drizzle is falling from a sky of fragmented, grayish cloud.

"Aunt Betty?"

"Yes?"

"Who will own this place when you die?"

She's shocked. The words are like a hard, stinging slap.

"Why? I—" She can't think of anything to say.

Edward is standing there looking at her, wearing those linen trousers that are almost impossible to iron. She feels the sudden threat of tears, backs away from him.

"Go inside and help your mother!" she barks, but he does not move: he just stands there looking into her eyes. His eyes are narrow and blue. She retreats, walks through the ruined garden, down the drive, and takes refuge in the woods, where she cannot be seen. She sits on a damp, mossy stone under the swaying trees for a long time, thinking.

For the first time since her father's death, she gives in to tears. Things come back to her: she sees herself at Christmas time wringing turkeys' necks, a mound of feathers at her feet; as a child running in to warm her hands at the fire and running out again, hearing her mother say, "She's such a hardy little girl." Her mother going out to the meadow, then laid out so unexpectedly, rosary beads entwined between her fingers. She sees Louisa in a gray suit leaving on the boat to England, coming back with a wealthy husband, pictures of babies in christening robes; her father taking pride in his grandson. She remembers Cyril Dawe sitting under the hawthorn in autumn with his arms around her, holding her tight, as though he was terrified she would get away. How he reached down and took a stone from under her, an act of tenderness. All her life she'd worked, she'd done the right things, but was it right? She sees herself stooping to pick up the pieces of a china plate her father broke in temper. Is this what she's become? A woman with broken plates? Is that all?

It seems to her now that there is nothing new under the sun. Edward thinks he'll step into her shoes, just as she stepped into her mother's. Inheritance is not renewal. More than anything, it keeps everything the same. All that is left, all that's sensible, is to clutch on to what is hers by right. Nothing shall ever stop her.

It is getting dark. How long has she been away? She walks up between the trees. She pacifies herself by concluding that it is only a matter of time before Louisa leaves. The children will have to be back to school in a few weeks. Come September, Betty will be able to get a good night's sleep, listen to the wireless, get rid of the dog hairs, cook when and what she likes, not have those awful children asking her what will happen when she dies.

When Betty arrives home, Louisa has spread a piece of blue cotton on the parlor floor, is putting an edge on her dressmaker's scissors with the file Betty keeps for sharpening knives.

"I was thinking we could make some new curtains for the bathroom. Those ones you have are ancient," she says. She puts the blade to the edge of the fabric and begins to cut.

"Do as you please," Betty says, and goes upstairs to lie down.

The weather does not let up in mid-August. Huge gray clouds provide a sullen parchment overhead. Frogs crawl in under the door on rainy nights, and Betty finds it almost impossible to get the clothes dry. She hangs them on a clotheshorse around the stove, lights the parlor fire, but a downdraft pushes black smoke into the room. She watches the bees robbing pollen from her crimson flowers outside the door, and counts the days.

She gets a lift into town with the insurance man and checks the balance in her bank account. Her money for August and September is used up. She takes money set aside for October and becomes imaginative with meals.

She is frying pancakes for tea one evening, the fat spattering lightly out on the draining board. The children are outside. The goslings have tried to follow the goose down the steps outside the front door, but their legs aren't long enough. They have fallen on their backs, their legs paddling the air. Ruth and Edward are turning them right side up with a long stick while the goose hisses at them and flaps her wings.

Louisa is sitting up next to the stove with a blanket around her shoulders.

"When will Stanley be coming?" Betty asks. She takes an enamel plate from the gas oven.

"I can't say."

"You can't say or you don't know?"

"I don't know."

"The children will have to be back in school in two weeks' time."

"Yes, I know."

"Well?"

"Well what?"

"Well, do you think he'll come before then?" Betty asks, and accidentally pours too much pancake batter into the pan.

"I don't know."

She watches the heat dimpling the edges of the batter, wondering how she'll turn it. "You've left Stanley."

"Those pancakes smell nice."

"You've left Stanley, and you think you can stay here."

"Would you like me to set the table?"

"Do you know that's the first time you've asked that since you arrived?" Betty has turned to face her.

"Is it? Edward! Ruth! Come on in for your tea!"

"Louisa!"

"I have a right to be here. It's in Daddy's will."

Ruth runs in.

"Wash your hands," Louisa says.

"I thought you said it was ready." Ruth says, staring at the empty table.

"It will be, love. Soon."

* * *

Louisa gets out of the kitchen that evening. She builds a small fire in the parlor, sits in the big armchair, and starts reading *War and Peace*. Betty goes out to milk the cow. She feels a strange, soothing mood of crystal clarity descend. It is all beginning to make sense. When she comes back inside, Louisa has taken a bath. She is sitting in front of the fireplace with her back to Betty, rubbing cold cream into her neck. Her hair is wrapped turbanlike in a towel. Two glasses on the mantel are filled to the brim with vodka.

"Are the children in bed?"

"Yes," Louisa says.

She hands a glass of vodka to Betty, as a peace offering, she supposes. They sip in silence while the light drains out of the day.

"Let me do your hair," says Betty suddenly. She goes upstairs for the comb. When she comes back, Louisa is sitting in front of the overmantel looking into the mirror.

Betty takes the comb from her apron pocket, gently removes the towel from Louisa's head, and begins to disentangle the knots in her hair. It is waist length, smelling strangely of fern and fruit.

"Nice shampoo."

"Yes."

Moonlight begins to shine brazenly through the french window. They can hear Edward snoring in the big room above their heads.

Betty pulls the comb's teeth through the damp, gold strands.

"It's like old times," Louisa says. "I wish I could go back. Do you ever wish that?"

"No. I'd just do the same things," Betty says.

"Yes. You're the clever one."

"Clever?"

"Poor old Betty, slaving away. You got what you wanted."

"Didn't you? A husband, children, a nice house. Father was no picnic."

A silence falls. The room seems unbearably quiet. Betty has been so busy, she has forgotten to wind the grandfather clock. A slice of winterish air slides in under the door.

"There are no satin curtains," Betty says.

"Whatever do you mean?"

"The dishwasher, the tumble dryer. You made it up. It's all made up."

"That isn't true."

Louisa is still admiring herself in the overmantel. She sits there like someone drugged, who cannot take her eyes off her reflection. She won't meet Betty's eyes in the mirror. She doesn't care that Betty did without, sent pound notes to her children, carried buckets through the yard, threw over a chance of marriage, spread dung, and washed her father's underpants for decades. She believes she can come and live here, encroach on Betty's ground, have her running around like a slave after her and her young family till the end of her days.

Betty reaches into her apron pocket. If Louisa feels the cold, high up on her neck, she doesn't react. She does not see the gleam of metal, the blades newly sharpened by her own hand. Betty holds the scissors, makes one swift cut. It takes only a second. Betty has great strength in her hands. She is still holding the scissors when Louisa, sensing the difference, sees her hair on the carpet.

Louisa is screaming and saying things, half truths. Something about greed and having a big house all to herself and not an ounce of sympathy. But Betty isn't listening anymore.

Louisa cries. She cries all night, while she packs, and all morning as she leads the children and the dog from the house. Betty says nothing. She just stands in the doorway looking out at the fine blue morning and smiles her terrible smile.

Louisa looks nothing without her hair.

The Scent of Winter

Whenever he thought about it afterward, Hanson never could say why he took the kids and the young nanny down to Greer's that Sunday. Greer was in a bad way, deep in something Hanson shouldn't have been next or near to. But the fact of the matter was he did go. And he did take the children.

It was a hot, fall day, but the evening wind had about it the scent of winter. It blew down casually from the north and shook summer out of the trees. Hanson left his wife, Lily, heavy with their third child, sleeping on the couch. He did not want to wake her, so he left a note, "Gone to Greer's, be back soon," with kisses Xed in pencil.

Hanson took it slow and drove with the windows down. The smell of burnt leaves, smoke from a fire, and something else, too, like burnt flesh, wafted into the station wagon. It made Hanson uneasy, but maybe it was just some farmer, burning a dead sheep. The boy whined and the nanny put her arm around him, read a story from a picture book about a heroic fireman as they drove. When Hanson slowed at a steel gate, the nanny took her cue, got out and opened it, and fastened it behind them. They turned into the long, dirt road, where a path of green weeds grew up between the tire marks. They passed a brick shed with a heavy, bolted door, quarter horses grazing inside a barbed-wire fence. Tall weeping shrubs shaded one side of the road, their limbs trailing across the windshield.

Ted Greer came down the back steps wearing a straw hat and shook Hanson's hand. He was a stocky man with muddy pants and a creased, white shirt. He smiled half-heartedly, showing teeth too straight to be real.

"Hey there," he said to the kids and mussed up their hair. "You guys want to throw a hook in the water?"

They carried fishing poles and the icebox down to the lake and stood on the white sand. The lake was silver as a nickel. Ted Greer reached into a feed bag and sprinkled food on the water's surface, and a barrage of hungry cat-fish thrashed the surface and gobbled up the pellets. The nanny undid the knots from the children's lines. They didn't need bait. The catfish snagged on the bare hooks, and the children pulled them onto the shore and watched them die.

"Must be up to three, maybe four pounds," said Hanson.

Greer nodded. "Must be."

The young nanny's heart wasn't in it. She was tired of coming to the country every weekend and catching fish they never ate. She was tired of working on Sundays. She told the kids to be careful of the hooks and slid most of the catch back into the water with her tennis shoe. The children grew bored. They scratched their mosquito bites and swore oh so softly.

"What's the matter with you, son?" asked Hanson. "Never seen a bug before?"

"He's tired, that's all," said the nanny. "He didn't take his nap."

They put some catfish in the icebox, and the nanny, sensing the men wanted to be alone, took the children for a walk.

"How is she holding up?" Hanson asked, when they were gone.

"The same."

"Did you get a doctor?"

"Doctors'll do no good. Doctors'll put her in a hospital and drug her up, and then she'll start talking, and Christ knows what'll happen if she talks."

"Have you told anybody about this . . . predicament you're in?"

"Predicament!" Greer shook his head. "You lawyers use the nicest words. That's what I was afraid of all along." He kicked something imaginary in the sand. "Hell, no, Charles, I haven't told a damn soul. I'm sorry I told you, getting you mixed up in all this. It's a real mess." Greer dumped what was left of the feed into the water, feed dust floated on the ripples. They stood there watching the fish fight each other for the food. They stood there a long time watching that until every speck of food was gone and the fish swam off into deeper water.

Greer's house was wooden, painted all over in custard yellow. A row of pecan trees shaded the back rooms. Sunlight broke through the leaves and threw crumpled, yellow shadows across the board floor. The kitchen smelled of ammonia and soup. Several half-empty, greasy plates stood on the countertops. Greer reached into the pantry shelf, and his hand fastened around the neck of a whiskey bottle. Hanson noticed all the empties in the garbage can.

"You been taking comfort in the bottle?"

Greer held his gaze. "You think maybe I should get a girl in?"

"Look, it really is none of my business. Just watch it doesn't make you careless, is all I'm saying."

He went to the window. The nanny was kneeling in the yard with his children, turning over something in the dirt.

Greer wiped sweat from his forehead.

"And how about him? Is he healing?"

"Oh, he's healing. The nigger's on the mend. My wife is starving herself to death, but there's no end to his appetite. He's fatter than a hog."

Hanson put his hand on Greer's shoulder, and for one terrified moment, thought Greer was going to cry. Instead, he turned and reached into the cupboard for two glasses. They were dusty, but he didn't rinse them under the tap.

"It's what happens after, what'll happen after, that's what's got me worried," Greer said. "I can't see any end to it, can't keep him locked up forever. There's only one ending now, far as I can see."

"You'll just have to make sure he doesn't talk."

"You ever know a nigger could hold his water?"

Hanson couldn't answer. There were things about Greer he never would understand; they never could see eye to eye on that one. They took the bottle into the living room and sat down. The armrests were frayed with years of arms resting. Above the mantelpiece was a framed photograph of a young Ronald Reagan, smiling, on a campaign trail.

"If it's a question of money—" Hanson started.

Greer shook his head. "Money'll only make it worse. No sir, money can't fix this one. I give him money, he'll come running back, looking for more." Greer looked into Hanson's eyes. "Oh, shit Charles, don't think I'm not grateful—"

"It's okay." Hanson dismissed it with a wave of his hand. "You're under a lot of pressure—"

"Pressure. Hell, sometimes I think I'm losing my mind."

The children were climbing the pecan trees, shaking the nuts, pop, pop, down onto the concrete outside the window. The nanny had a rock in her hand. Hanson heard her say they had to be careful, to crack the shell without smashing the pecan. She was always telling them to be careful.

The men drank in silence. A clock ticked on the wall, ticked slow like the battery was low. Hanson looked up at the clock. Suddenly, he stood up.

"Can I see her, Ted? I'd like to see her."

"It'll do no good," said Greer.

"If I can see her, then maybe I can understand."

Greer put his head in his hands. Hanson looked into his whiskey, watched the ice melt while Greer composed himself. A little bubble burst on the surface of his drink. Several minutes passed. Greer put his hand in his pocket and took out a silver key. He swallowed the rest of his drink and got up. There was blood on his throat where he'd nicked himself shaving. His hands were anything but steady. Hanson wondered if that's what a man looked like going to his execution. He supposed it was.

Greer led the way down a carpeted hallway to a door. He knocked softly, twice, then unlocked the door. Inside smelled strange and sour, not like anything human. The room was dim. On the wall above the bed hung a color photograph of a woman with her hand cupping the muzzle of a bay Morgan horse. Beneath it lay the woman, drastically altered, her elbows sharp as hinges. The arms were doll-like, bruised. Greer's wife couldn't have weighed more than seventy pounds.

Greer sat on the bed and took one of her hands in his.

"Hey, my little lady," he whispered. He patted her head.

Slowly, she turned her back on them and brought her knees up to her chin. Nobody said anything.

When they came out to the other room, Hanson said, "Whatever you gave him, it wasn't enough."

"Tell that to a court of law," said Greer.

"I would have if you had given me the chance."

Greer sat down like he was made of lead. Hanson heard the wicker strain.

"I should have shot him, but it's too late now. I just didn't have it in me," said Greer. "I could have claimed self-defense. Now the law's gonna come down on me.

Most of the time I think I should've got the police. I really do. He'd have done time, real time, if I'd got a decent law-yer, somebody like you. But I look at her, my own wife, starving herself to death in that room, and I know I wouldn't be satisfied. Someday, maybe a couple months from now, I'd go down to the store and he'd be sitting out there, drinking Coca-Cola on the porch, out loose, a free man again. Nobody does time anymore. There's no jus-tice. Whatever happened to justice in this country? That's what I'd like to know."

Hanson was silent. Healthy, lilac sunlight was sliding through the trees. Hanson wanted to get out—it was a mistake to come—but he waited for Greer to make some move to allow him to take his leave. The blind flapped, was sucked in by the draft.

"Don't judge me, Charles. Don't you judge me. Can you look me in the eye and tell me you'd do any different if some Negro came and did that to your wife, if some guy broke into your house and raped Lily?"

Hanson didn't answer.

"Well?"

"No," said Hanson, truthfully. "I can't."

When Hanson called the children to go home, there was no answer. He went outside and called their names and the nanny's name, but all he heard was his own voice and the wind in the trees. He looked at Greer. Greer looked up the dusty road. They ran out and got in the truck and drove and knew, when they saw them, that it was too late.

The steel door on the shed was open. Greer hadn't put the padlock on.

"Jesus Christ!" said Hanson.

In the near distance, up ahead, a young black man, blinded by daylight, was running as fast as he could across the fields toward the highway. The nanny was screaming, and the kids were screaming too, running and screaming. The men caught the children like wild animals just about a hundred yards from the shed and bundled them up and held them, panting, in their arms. The nanny screamed, "I quit! I quit! You goddamn, sons-a-barbarian-bitches!" and ran in the direction of the Negro, leaving the men holding the children.

The Burning Palms

Every morning the boy dresses and leaves the house before his father wakes. It's an uphill walk for the first mile, until he reaches the old school. From there he can see her cottage in the valley, the thatched roof glistening in the wet sun. The wheat in the surrounding fields is past ripe. Farmers are waiting for fine weather to bring out the combines and save the harvest. It was a bad summer.

His grandmother's cottage is not like other houses. There's no pretty garden out front to turn people's heads, no flower beds to weed or lawn to mow. It looks worse now than ever it did; the narrow strip of ground is littered with builder's rubble of warped boards, lime bags, and broken glass. The council wanted to knock the house down in April, but his grandmother would have none of it, told them it was her house, and she would do as she pleased. The boy was there the day the county engineer came out to persuade her.

"Look, missus," he said, "we'll build you a grand new house somewhere else with a little bathroom and electricity. A snug house for your old age."

"Who says I'll live to be old?" she said. (She's almost eighty.)

The engineer smiled. "Well, with the help of God, you will, and wouldn't it be nice not to be dragging well water for the rest of your days?"

"There's no water makes tea like well water. Would ya not agree?"

"Ah now, missus—"

"Would ya like a cup of tea?"

"You must see reason—"

"Whose reason? There's no point in reasoning over something I don't want. Is there? Is there?"

The county engineer had no answer.

So, instead of knocking the house down, the council built a tall, block wall between the cottage and the road. Now nobody can see out, or in. The front rooms are dark and gloomy, and the new plaster in the front half of the house isn't painted. It's the strangest-looking house in the parish.

The boy opens the gate and runs down to the back door. Her kitchen smells of burnt lard, coal smoke, and lamp oil. He fills the teapot from the water bucket, gets her china cup and saucer off the dresser. His mother used saucers, but now his father makes do with mugs and doesn't bother with a tablecloth. His Sunday clothes aren't pressed; his shoes don't shine the way they did before.

He knocks on her back bedroom door, puts her tea on the dressing table. She's wide awake. She doesn't sleep much, keeps odd hours; but always she waits for him to bring her tea before she rises. Lately, there's a shake in her hands she can't control. She isn't able to carry a cup on a saucer without spilling the tea, but the boy has learned to pretend he doesn't notice these things. He opens the window to drive out the smell of the chamber pot. The glass in these windows is blurred, the view's distorted. A photograph taken on his mother's wedding day is hanging crooked on the wall, his mother and father in dark suits smiling for the camera. His grandmother did not come to the wedding because she did not approve of his mother marrying his father.

His grandmother was a gypsy woman once but settled here when the boy's mother was born. Before that she traveled Ireland collecting scrap with her husband. The boy vaguely remembers his grandfather. A big man who lifted him up onto the bare back of a chestnut mare and laughed when he was frightened.

"I was dreaming about cattle," she says, and blows on her tea.

"We'll finish the job today, Gran."

"Aye, I won't be sorry."

They have been trying to finish the wallpapering all summer, but their hearts aren't in it. They wind up digging new potatoes in the plot behind the house, frying black pudding and playing Beggar-the-Knave, listening to the rain dripping on the rhubarb leaves. Most days she sends the boy down to the shop on the bicycle, gives him some of her pension money for sweets and her tobacco. Then the van comes round on Fridays with the groceries and gas.

The boy takes the chamber pot from under the bed and empties it down the plot, rinsing it out with rainwater from the tank. He looks at his reflection in the water's surface. His fringe is growing down over his eyes: he needs a haircut.

There's not much wallpapering left in the front bedroom, three or four strips, a few awkward patches around the window. They used to call this Mammy's room. This is where she slept; this was her room until she married the boy's father and moved into the big house up the road. They hung the first strip crooked but carried on, and now the palm trees in the pattern are leaning to the left. Outside, a gust blows the garden gate open, and an empty lime bag cartwheels in the breeze. The boy must thin the paste; he must finish wallpapering today because this is the end of summer. Tomorrow he must go back to school. He does not want to think about school because it reminds him of homework and Saint Patrick's Day.

Saint Patrick's morning came white with frost. His father sent him back into the house for water to melt ice on the windscreen. His mother pinned a shamrock on his collar, gave him a 10p coin for the collection box. She wore her good tweed suit, her linen blouse. The boy could smell her Apple Blossom perfume in the car on the way to mass. He liked his mother's perfume and the silver, frosted trees, gliding past. At mass, they sang hymns in Irish: "Dochas Linn Naomh Padraig!" Even the old men standing down at the confession boxes sang along with that one. The voices rose as one toward the lofty chapel ceiling. During the sermon he looked at the stations of the cross on the chapel walls, followed the story of the crucifixion. Afterward his father dropped them off at his grandmother's house, but he refused to come in for tea. He was in a hurry, he said. The races were on in Coolattin.

"Will I call for ye on the way home?"

"It'll be too late." His mother knew he'd be the worse for drink. "We'll walk."

His mother stuffed a chicken and iced a sponge cake with green, runny icing. The boy went to the well for drinking water, balanced the milk can on the old steel push-chair his father'd made for him when he was just a child. He liked feeling useful, liked the greedy sound of the bucket glug-glugging the well water, and then the shrill spill into the milk can, wheeling it back along the icy road, and the frost shimmering like tinsel on the hedges.

Back in the kitchen, the blustery trees made a carousel of shadow. There were smells of baking and cauliflower cheese, and a woman was singing on the transistor radio. His mother set the table, used the good china, the bone-handled knives. After dinner she read the *Nationalist* while the boy did his homework. There was spelling and some math. He hated math; it didn't always make sense. How could a minus by a minus be a plus? Geography was his subject. He could name all the counties in Ireland, the mountains, the rivers, their tributaries, the capital towns.

Toward dusk, his mother braided his grandmother's hair into a white plait. Flames from the black range threw shadows on the linoleum, and his grandmother sprinkled oatmeal on the window ledges for the birds. Looking back, the boy would like to believe that nobody wanted to leave, that nobody wanted to put an end to that day. But that's not what happened.

"Okay, son, finish up. It's getting dark."

"Ah, Mam!" The boy had finished his homework, was reading about the formation of cliffs in his geography book.

"I'm tired out, son."

"I'm not finished with my homework," he lied.

He lied because he did not want to go home. His father would come home drunk after gambling the housekeeping. They would fight again about money.

"How long more?" his mother asked.

"I've geography to do still. Ages."

"Well, I might have a lie-down. But wake me when you're finished."

She went into the front bedroom and closed the door.

The boy sat reading, drew diagrams of the sea cutting into the land and the land falling off into the ocean. He read in the withering light until the print grew indistinct and he had to hold the pages toward the window to see the words. His grandmother didn't like to light the lamp until it was necessary, for that, she said, marked the end of another day. Dusk was her time. She rolled her daily cigarette and sat smoking, staring at the west-facing window until the sun sank.

"You'll destroy your eyes, love."

She got up and adjusted the wick on the oil lamp and struck the match, lowered the shade down over the flame, bathed the room in sudden, gauzy lamplight.

"Get the cake tin," she said. "We'll make a cupán tae."

They ate slabs of sponge cake, played Forty-five, kept track of the score with matchsticks. The boy remembers red, burning coals keeping the cold at bay, the shuffling of cards, cinders collapsing in the grate, the smell of paraffin, the sudden roars of cars passing close by on the road, people coming home from the races, the constant rush of wheels on the tarmacadam.

The boy was winning when it happened. Two tricks to win, and he had the knave. His grandmother was robbing the queen. Then the crash, the sound of breaking glass and falling stone. At first the boy thought a tree had fallen on the roof.

"What in the name of God?"

"Mammy!" the boy cried.

When his grandmother opened the front bedroom door, a cloud of plaster dust fell into the passage. At first they couldn't see, but the transport lorry still had one headlight working. It had run off the road, had come right through the front wall into the bedroom. In the wreckage, his grandmother found his mother. She was crushed between the lorry and the wall. The boy saw blood. He didn't want to look. His mother's hand was hanging lifeless like one of the dummies in Duffy's shop.

"Margaret!"

The driver's face was slumped over the wheel. More blood. A horse groaning. Strangers ran in with torches. Ages passed. A siren grew close and stopped. A uniformed man came in and pumped his mother's chest, and breathed air into her mouth with his own. When he shook his head, somebody led the boy from the room. He was taken out of the house, under the trees, and people told him everything would be all right. Later he heard the shot of a gun as the horse was put down.

There was ice on the road that night. One skid on the bend was all it took. There was nothing to prevent it happening. Some people said it was a miracle it hadn't happened years ago, what with the house being so close to the road. It was an accident waiting to happen, they said.

Strange, dreamlike days followed. Grown men shook the boy's hand, as if he too was a man. Women came into his mother's house and made sandwiches and filled cups with tea and did the washing up and put the dishes back where they did not belong. People stood around drinking and smoking in the parlor, dragging dirt in on their shoes, onto his mother's good sheepskin rug, saying what a fine woman she was. Was. People talking about his mother in the past tense, as if she was dead. But she *was* dead, the boy had to remind himself. His mother was dead.

The boy found his father in the forge after the burial. He was standing there in his Sunday clothes, curving a red-hot iron bar, making hinges to hang a gate. A half-empty whiskey bottle was standing on the shelf where he kept the tools.

"Well, son," he said, "I don't know how we'll manage now your mother's gone."

When the boy didn't answer, his father started pumping life into the fire with the bellows.

The boy went outside and looked up at the stars. His mother had said the stars were angels looking down at them. His mother believed in God. People said his mother was in heaven. He couldn't go back inside. The house was full and empty at the same time. There were snowdrops she'd arranged in a vase, a shirt she'd ironed and left for him on a wooden hanger, her furry slippers under the armchair.

The boy ran across the fields, left the track of his good shoes in the fresh clay. His heart was hammering; he was breathing hard, sweating, when he reached the cottage. The place was in a shambles. His grandmother was sitting in the rubble with a blanket around her shoulders, drinking brandy from a cup. Her hair was loose. She looked wild.

"If you'd gone home when you were told," she said, "your mother would be alive today."

His grandmother is smoking a lot now, stops every time they hang a strip of paper to roll a cigarette. Her hands are shakier than usual. There's a little trail of tobacco on the floor between the kitchen and his mother's bedroom. The palm trees look queer and out of place on these walls. It was painted a solid green before.

The boy pastes the wall while his grandmother pastes the paper. Slap slap, say the brushes. The last strip won't

[149]

fit into the corner. The palm trees are crooked. When the boy slides them into place at the bottom, they overlap at the top. He cannot fix it. *Wake me when you're finished.* He feels hot and cold at the same time. *If you'd gone home when you were told.* Tomorrow he must go back to school. She would have covered his books with wallpaper, inked his name on the collar of his new anorak. She would fry mashed potatoes, wash his lunch box, and sign the exercise book to say he'd done his homework. She would ask him to go out and make sure the latch was on the gate, fill his hot water bottle, and say, "Sleep tight," at bedtime.

The wallpapering is done. His grandmother is tidying up the last strip, cutting away the excess at the skirting board with a blade. Her hands are shaking, and the cut she makes is jagged. She sits down and rolls a cigarette. Tobacco falls into her lap. The boy strikes the match for her. It is getting on for dusk; light is draining from the day. The palm trees look like a storm has blown them sideways.

"It's crooked, Gran."

"No matter. Who's to see?" She is staring out the window at the council wall.

"We'll make a bonfire." There's fire in her eyes.

They collect the scraps and rags and take them outside. She gets the oil can and the sprong from the shed, and they collect all the rubbish, make a pile out front beside the wall. She douses broken ceiling boards with lamp oil and strikes the match. A blaze starts. Smoke rises. Broken branches crackle in the heat; bark turns into white ash. This wood smoke smells good. It stirs something ancient and necessary in the boy's heart. He won't go home. He will live here all winter, make fires and play cards and draw well water and go to the shop. He will not leave his grandmother.

She is pulling withered boughs out of the ditch, pitching them onto the flames. She can't get the fire big enough.

Smoke drifts out across the wall, rouses the drowsy wasps in the fuchsia bushes at the far side of the road. Crows are circling in the sky. Caw. Caw. The Irish sound for where. Ca? Ca? they ask. Beyond the fire, the evening seems much darker; shadows are wrestling at their feet. His grandmother's feet are big, his mother's shoes wouldn't fit her. He watches her lighting the cement bag in the fire. Something in his blood tells him what she'll do. But he is stunned when she pitches it onto the thatch.

"Granny!" He feels like laughing.

"Stay there."

She goes inside. Windows open. She comes out carrying her good coat, her pension book, his mother's wedding photo. She ignites a ribbon of lamp oil in the cottage. It doesn't take long for the parlor curtains to catch fire. The wallpaper is burning, the palm trees are alight, and the thatch is ablaze when the old woman takes the boy's arm. They start walking, turn the bend. There is only one place to go. The boy faces it. Debris from the house, little bits of lighted straw, pieces of the past, are traveling through the air. The road is dark, too dark to see ahead. When they reach the old school, they stop and look back at the house burning in the valley. The dead pines at the gable end are blazing. A combine harvester's headlights are moving through the wheat fields.

"It's a strange day for the harvest," the boy says, to break the silence. He can feel rain in the air: drizzle will soon fall.

"Well, if they don't do it now, they'll never do it," his grandmother says, and leans on him all the way back to his father.

Passport Soup

Frank Corso has come to expect nothing. He comes home late to an empty house without fire. Tonight he gathers kindling, lights the furnace, and warms his hands. For supper he fries bacon and green tomatoes and lays a place for one. His wife is hardly ever home. When she is home, she is sitting on the veranda, staring out with expectation at the asphalt road, waiting for the phone to ring. Tonight is normal. Her station wagon is missing from the carport. She is probably driving along the highway, searching.

He takes a carton from the refrigerator and fills a cup with milk. He butters a slice of rye bread and cuts his bacon into small pieces. It's then he notices the photograph on the milk carton. It is a photograph of a young girl wearing dungarees. There is a gap at the front of her smile where she lost a tooth. MISSING, it reads in big, faint letters underneath. *Elizabeth Corso, aged nine. Disappeared from her home outside Boulder, Colorado, on September 9th. Last seen wearing a red sweatshirt and blue jeans. If you have seen this person, please call . . .* and a phone number for the police station that Frank Corso has long since committed to memory.

He remembers the night Elizabeth lost that tooth. He told her to put it under her pillow, said the tooth fairy would take it and leave a gift. He'd put a dollar bill under there after she'd gone to sleep, but he forgot to take the tooth.

"Daddy! Daddy!" was what she said the next morning. "The tooth fairy came!"

Frank has lost his appetite. He pushes his plate aside and gets up and puts the milk carton with his daughter's photograph back in the refrigerator and goes to bed. The sheets are cold. He hears a wedge of snow sliding from the eaves of the roof onto the drift beneath the window. Daylight bleaches the bedroom walls before he finally falls into a shallow sleep.

That was Monday.

On Tuesday, when he gets home, his wife's station wagon is parked in the drive. She is in the girl's room. He can hear her in there. She has wound up the music in the girl's jewelry box. He knows she is in there on the girl's bed watching the little plastic ballerina turning on its spring, tormenting herself. He pushes the door ajar and looks in. His wife stares right through him, past him, as if there is a picture behind him he is preventing her from seeing. He has become the invisible husband.

"Hey," he says.

He approaches, sits on the bed, and puts his hand on her knee. She flings it off the way she would fling a snake off her lap, picks up the jewelry box, and walks out of the room. When Frank comes out to the den, he can see her sitting on the veranda, can hear the music slowing as the spring loosens. Tonight, he does not bother with supper. He takes a bottle of scotch from the liquor cabinet into the bedroom with the newspaper. He reads the headlines, the sports, and the obituaries, goes into the bathroom and sits on the toilet. When he looks up, hanging there on the wall is an enlarged photograph of his daughter that was not there yesterday. It is a picture taken of her as flower girl at his sister-in-law's wedding. She is wearing a pink, satin dress that comes down to her toes, satin-covered toes peeping out from underneath her dress. In her hands she holds a bouquet of white roses wreathed in baby's breath. Frank sits there on the toilet and puts his face in his hands, and weeps.

On Wednesday when he comes home, there's no sign of her car, but the furnace is lit, and there's a note that reads: "Gone to Mom's. Be back soon." She has not left a note like that since before Elizabeth went missing. He takes heart in the note, runs a hot bath, and gets into his dressing gown. He opens the door of Elizabeth's room. It is exactly as she left it. He looks into her closet, slides the wooden hangers to the left, then to the right. He remembers her wearing these clothes; at least he thinks he remembers. He sniffs the underarm of a yellow sweater: nothing. He takes a coloring book from a shelf and turns the pages; it is an old book from the time before she could keep the crayon inside the lines. Frank lies down on the bed and lifts the receiver of the Mickey Mouse telephone, wonders whom he can call. There is nobody. People lost contact with him; nobody knew what to say. He puts the receiver down and listens to the icy wind hustling the trees outside the window. He thinks of Elizabeth being out in that. He hopes, if she is alive, that she is not out in that weather. He would rather his little girl were dead than be out in a night like tonight.

"God forgive me," he says.

He is beginning to believe in God.

Suddenly, he is standing in the cornfield where he lost her, looking for her, calling her name: "Elizabeth! Elizabeth!" She is running, running down from the drown-deep, river water's edge, toward him. He is happy. He can hear her running, out of breath. Then another voice comes from somewhere else, also calling her name. She turns back, away from her father, and follows the other voice. The man who owns this voice steps into view. A black stranger grips her hand. Her father shouts and tells her to stop, but she keeps walking away from him. He can see a mountain lion's footprints in the dry earth. His voice gets harsh, harsher. But she keeps walking away. All the cells in his body are bumping together, telling his brain to move, move, but he cannot. He watches her going away with the stranger making promises, and then the whole thing fades, becomes part of the silence beyond the cornfield and the river.

Frank wakes with a start in the dark of his daughter's bedroom to the ringing of the telephone. He picks up the receiver, but no one speaks. It is his wife. He knows it is his wife. He can hear her, breathing, can feel her hatred traveling through the line, into the room.

"Bad dreams?" she asks and hangs up. He hears her hanging up in the other room, on the other line. He gets up and goes back into what used to be their bedroom so she can lie down in what has become hers.

Frank Corso lost his own child in his own field at the back of his own house. Those are the facts. At one point in that late evening she was there, and then she wasn't. It was that simple and that hard. The police came, detectives who asked questions:

"Did you have an argument?"

"Could you tell us, once again, Mr. Corso, exactly what happened?"

"Take your time. These things happen."

They stood there with their little black notebooks and cigarettes. There was suspicion in their eyes. Frank gave them the same, unsatisfactory answers. Then came the search party, neighbors walking every inch of those fields, through the rows of corn, the meadow, and the grassland where the cattle grazed. It grew dark. Rows of flashlight beams crossed the land, shone into ditches, hedges, into the limbs of trees. But nobody found her. Not even the men in scuba gear who immersed themselves in water and dragged the river for her body.

When Frank Corso pulls his sheet back, there are photographs, twelve, fifteen, twenty-two photographs. Elizabeth sitting on his knee, Elizabeth at her grandmother's,

Elizabeth swinging in a rubber tire, Elizabeth with her mother's arms around her, sitting backward on her pony, at Disneyland, blowing out birthday candles. He gathers the photographs carefully and puts them in the sock drawer and lies down.

On Thursday, Frank does not come home. He leaves the office, gets Chinese to go, and books into a motel room on Airline Highway. He props himself up with pillows and eats with a plastic fork and watches TV. He flicks through the channels—a talk show with some guy who was dead for a while on the operating table, a documentary about the First World War, some woman talking about how to train your dogs to sit and fetch and heel. He settles for the war, watches till it's over, and then he thinks about leaving his wife. A big part of him wants to leave. The house feels like a morgue. All that blame and guilt and silence. Except for those two words, "bad dreams," last night, his wife has not addressed him since late September. But there is a chance, a small, irretrievable chance that Elizabeth will come home, and, if she does, Frank will be there. She could be there now. She could have walked into the cold house with snow melting in her hair, asking where Daddy is. He dials the number. His wife picks up the phone.

"Hello."

"Hello," he says. "Just called to say I'm staying out tonight. I was just wondering, you know, I was just wondering—"

The line goes dead.

Passport Soup

* * *

On Friday, not only is the furnace hot when Frank comes home, but there's a big pot of soup simmering on the stove, warm bread in a basket on the table. He takes his coat off and shakes the snow off his pants, wipes his shoes on the mat. His wife is setting the table. Three forks, three knives, three soup spoons, cut-glass tumblers. Frank sits down and looks at her. She is all dressed up, wearing a blue evening dress, down to her toes. He's seen it before, but he can't say where. He recognizes the necklace, the big opal he bought her for their first wedding anniversary when she was pregnant. It dips down into the valley between her breasts. The ordeal has dimmed the luster in her hair, and she's thinner now, but she's still a handsome woman.

"What's going on?"

"I made supper," she says. "How was your day?"

He had almost forgotten the sound of her old voice.

"Are you expecting company?"

"How about a drink?" she asks. "I feel like a drink. How about you?"

"Sure," he says. "I'll—"

"No," she says. "I'll fix it, honey. Why don't you change?"

He goes into the bedroom and undoes the knot in his tie, his shoelaces. He changes into jogging pants, a turtleneck sweater, finds his slippers. He pulls back the duvet, but there are no photographs between the sheets. When he goes back out into the kitchen, his wife is taking warm

[159]

soup bowls from the oven with a cloth. She hands him a tumbler of Wild Turkey with a napkin around the glass and turns off the overhead light. She puts a stick of butter on a dish and takes a ladle from a drawer. She stands before him and takes the lid off. A thick, curling steam rises between them. She smiles. When she leans over to ladle out the soup, he looks down the front of her dress. Her breasts are straining against her dress. He takes a sip of whiskey. He feels like a husband again. Maybe everything will be all right. Maybe they can overcome this. Maybe they can have another child.

"This smells good," he says and reaches for his soup spoon once she's seated. Then he looks into his bowl. He puts his spoon down. He starts counting, counts to nine. Floating on the surface of his soup are nine passport photos of Elizabeth, smiling in a booth. He pushes the bowl away and puts his head down on his arms.

"Speciality of the house: passport soup," his wife says.

"Stop it!"

"What's the matter, Frank? Don't you like it? You never did appreciate my cooking."

Not until Frank throws the bowl of soup against the wall does her voice change, does she really start talking.

"You bastard. Telling Elizabeth about fairies, making her believe in all that crap. You lost her, Frank, you lost her! You lost our child. You useless, son of a bitch!"

She walks across the floor and slaps him, hard, with the back of her hand. Then she does it again. Frank gets down on his knees. He is kneeling before her. He holds on to the hem of her dress. Her dress is blue. He pinches the fabric between his fingers. He begs her forgiveness. She does not forgive him. She may never forgive him. She backs away. He hears blame, razor-sharp words flying like knives across the room, across his head. The words slice through him. It is the truth. She is tearing him asunder, putting the knife in; she is twisting the knife and taking pleasure in twisting it.

But Frank Corso feels better. It is a start. It is better than nothing.

Close to the Water's Edge

Tonight he is out on the balcony, his dark tan stunning against the white of his dress shirt. Many days have passed since he left Cambridge, Massachusetts, to spend time at his mother's penthouse on the coast. He does not care for these rooms, with its vicious swordfish mounted on the walls and all these mirrors that make it impossible to do even the simplest thing without seeing his reflection.

He stays out on the beach and through his shades watches the bathers, the procession of young men with washboard bellies walking the strand. Women turn over on their deck chairs browning themselves evenly on all sides. They come here with their summer books and sunhats, reaching into their coolers for beer and Coppertone. In the afternoons when the heat becomes unbearable, he swims out to the sandbar, a good half mile from the shore. He can see it now, the strip of angry waves breaking in the shallows. Now the tide is advancing, erasing the white, well-trodden sands. A brown pelican, a small piece of the past, floats by on the Texas wind. Joggers stay close to the water's edge, their shadows fastened like guardians at their sides.

Inside, his mother is arguing with his stepfather, the millionaire who owns these condominiums. After his parents divorced, his mother said that people have no control over who they fall in love with, and soon afterward married the millionaire. Now he can hear them talking, their enraged whispers gathering speed on the slope of their argument. It is an old story.

"I'm warning you, Richard, don't bring it up!"

"Who brought it up? Who?"

"It's his birthday, for Christ's sake!"

"Who said anything?"

The young man looks down. At the hot tub, a mother braces herself and enters the steamy waters. Screams from racing children pierce the air. He feels the same trepidation he always feels at these family occasions, and wonders why he came back here when he could be in Cambridge in his T-shirt and shorts, drinking his Australian beer, playing chess on the computer. He takes the cufflinks from his pocket, a gift his grandmother gave him shortly before she died. They are gold-plated cufflinks whose gold is slowly wearing off, revealing the steel underneath.

When his grandmother first married, she begged her husband to take her to the ocean. They were country people, pig farmers from Tennessee. His grandmother said she had never laid eyes on the Atlantic. She said if she saw the ocean, she could settle down. It wasn't anything she could explain. But each time she asked her husband, his response was the same.

"Who'll feed the pigs?"

"We could ask the neighbors—"

"You can't trust anybody. That's our livelihood out there."

Months passed; she grew heavy with child and finally gave up asking to see the ocean. Then one Sunday her husband shook her awake.

"Pack a bag, Marcie," he said, "we're going to the coast."

It wasn't yet light when they got into the car. They drove all that day, across the hills of Tennessee toward Florida. The landscape changed from green, hilly farmland to dry acres with tall palms and pampas grass. The sun was going down when they arrived. She got out and gasped at the Atlantic, whose end she could not see. It looked green in the evening sun. It wasn't what she expected. It seemed a lonely, infertile place to her, with the stink of seaweed and the gulls fighting for leftovers in the sand.

Then her husband took out his pocket watch.

"One hour, Marcie. I'll give you one hour," he said. "If you're not back by then, you can find your own way home."

She walked for half an hour with her bare feet in the frothy edge of the sea, then turned back along the cliff path, and from the shelter of some trees, watched her husband, at five minutes past the appointed hour, slam the car door and turn the ignition. Just as he was gathering speed, she jumped into the road and stopped the car.

[164]

Then she climbed in and spent the rest of her life with a man who would have gone home without her.

His nineteenth birthday is marked by a dinner at Leonardo's, the fancy seafood restaurant overlooking the bay. His mother, dressed in a white pants suit with a rhinestone belt, joins him on the balcony.

"I'm so proud of you, honey."

"Mom," he says and embraces her. She's a small woman with a hot temper. She gazes out at the water.

"Will you fix my tie?" he asks. "I never could do this right."

She knots the silk into an unnecessarily tight bow.

"There," she says. "You'll be the belle of the ball. How many mothers can say, 'My boy's going to Harvard University?' I'm a pig farmer's daughter from Tennessee, and my boy is going to Harvard. When I'm low, I always remember that, and it cheers me up no end."

"Mom!"

"You play your cards right and this could all be yours someday," she says. "He's got no kids. You wonder why I married him, but I was thinking of you all along."

Just then the millionaire comes out with a lighted cigar and blows a mouthful of smoke into the night. He's an ordinary-looking man with the whitest teeth money can buy.

"You-all ready? I could eat a small child," he says.

The restaurant owner greets the millionaire, escorts them to the table. A wooden board of crab claws is brought

Claire Keegan

out. The millionaire eats them with his bare hands and clicks his fingers for the waiter, who pops a champagne cork. He always drinks champagne.

"Did you hear about this guy Clinton? Says if he's elected president, he's gonna let queers into the military," he says. "What do you think of that, Harvard?"

"Richard," his mother says.

"It's okay, Mom. Well, I don't think—"

"What's next? Lesbians coaching the swim team, running for the Senate?"

"Richard!"

"What kind of defense would that be? A bunch of queers! We didn't win two world wars that way. I don't know what this country is turning into."

Smells of horseradish and dill spill out from the kitchen. A lobster has got loose in the tank, but the waiter dips a net into the water and traps him.

"No more politics," his mother says. "It's my boy's night. He got a 3.75 grade point average last semester. Now what do you think of that, Richard?"

"3.75? Not bad."

"Not bad? Well, I should say not! He's top of his class at Harvard!"

"Mom."

"No, I won't be hushed up this time! He's top of the class, and he's nineteen years old today! A grown man, almost. Let's have a toast."

"Now, there's an idea," says the millionaire. He refills the champagne flutes. "Here's to the brightest young man in the whole state of Florida," he says. (They are smiling now, suddenly at ease. There is a chance that this dinner will not be like the others.) ". . . and to not having queers in the military!"

The mother's smile capsizes. "Goddamn, Richard!"

"What's the matter? It's just a little joke. Doesn't anybody around here know how to take a joke anymore?"

The waiter arrives with a steel tray and the entrées. Turbot for the lady, salmon for the young man, and lobster for the millionaire. The millionaire wants more champagne.

"There must be some fine women up there at Harvard," he says. "Some real knockouts."

"They accept us on the basis of intelligence, not looks."

"Even so. The best and the brightest. How come you never bring a girl down?" The millionaire ties a napkin around his neck, takes the pincers and breaks a claw open, picks out the meat. "They must be all around you like flies," he says, "a young man like you. Why, when I was your age I had a different woman every weekend."

"These olives!" the mother says. "Taste these olives!"

They eat in silence for the rest of the meal, as the millionaire likes to concentrate on his food. Afterward, the maitre d' comes by and whispers a few words into the millionaire's ear. The lights around their table are doused, and a lighted cake is carried from the kitchen by a nervous, Mexican waiter singing "Happy Birthday." It is a pink cake, the pinkest cake the young man has ever seen, like a cake you'd have at a christening party for twin girls. The millionaire is grinning.

[167]

"Make a wish, honey!" his mother says.

The young man closes his eyes and makes a wish, then blows hard, extinguishing the candles. The millionaire takes the knife and carves it into uneven pieces, like a pie chart. The young man stuffs a piece into his mouth, licks the frosting. The millionaire reaches for his mother's hand, clasps her jeweled fingers.

"Happy birthday, son," the mother says and kisses him on the mouth. He tastes lipstick, stands, and he hears himself thanking them for a pleasant birthday. He hears his mother calling his name, the waiter saying, "Good evening, sir," at the doorway. He is crossing the highway now, finding a space between the speeding cars. Other college kids are drinking beer on the promenade, watching the bungee jumpers throwing themselves into midair, screaming.

Down at the deserted beach, the tide has reclaimed the strand. The water is rough in the night wind. He loosens the knot at his throat and walks on and on, losing track of time. Up at the pier, yachts with roped-in sails stand trembling on the water. He thinks of his grandmother coming to the ocean. She said if she had her life to live again, she would never have climbed back into that car. She'd have stayed behind and turned into a streetwalker sooner than go home. Nine children she bore him. When her grandson asked what made her get back in, her answer was, "Those were the times I lived in. That's what I believed. I thought I didn't have a choice."

His grandmother, with whom he lived while his parents broke up, the woman who embraced him so tight she bruised him, is dead now. Not a day has passed when he has not felt her absence. She is dead, but he is nineteen years old, and alive and inhabiting space on the earth, getting As at Harvard, walking on a beach in the moonlight without any time constriction. He will never marry; he knows that now. The water looks like liquid pewter. He kicks his shoes off and, barefooted, enters the salty waters. The white waves that mark the sandbar are clearly visible in the darkness. He feels dirty, smells the cigar smoke on his clothes. He strips naked, placing the cufflinks safely in his pants pocket, and leaves his clothes on the strand. When he wades into the big white-fringed waves, the water is a cold surprise. He swims, feels clean again. Perhaps he will leave tomorrow, call the airline, change his flight, go back to Cambridge.

When he reaches the white waves, he is relieved. The water is deeper, the waves angrier now that it is night. He can rest here before the return swim to the shore. He lowers his feet to feel the sand. Waves thrash over his head, knocking him back into the deep water. He cannot find solid ground. His heart is beating fast, he swallows water, goes farther out to find the shallowest place. He never meant to drink all that champagne. He never meant to go swimming in the first place. All he wanted was to wash the evening off him. He struggles for the longest time, goes underwater, believing it will be easier if he comes up only for air. He sees the lighted condominiums on the shore. Out of nowhere comes the thought of his grandmother, who after coming all that way, and with only an hour to spend, would not get into the water, even though she was a strong, river swimmer. When he asked her why, she said she just didn't know how deep it was. Where the deep started, or where it ended. The young man floats on the surface, then slowly makes his way back to the lighted condominiums on the shore. It is a long way off, but the penthouse lights are clear against the sky. When he reaches the shallow water, he crawls on his belly and collapses on the sand. He is breathing hard and looking around for his clothes, but the tide has taken them away. He imagines the first species that crawled out of the sea, the amount of courage it took to sustain life on land. He thinks of the young men in Cambridge, his stepfather saying Harvard, like Harvard is his name, his mother's diamonds winking like fake stars, and his wish for an ordinary life.

You Can't Be Too Careful

Jeremiah Ezekiel Devereux is my name. My old man was a Bible freak, but we won't go into that here. People just call me Jay. Butch did too, but I don't suppose that matters now. I was born October 9, 1943, in Baton Rouge General and we moved to 16 Kramen Street, Confuscius, when I was five years old. I've been living there ever since.

The first time I saw Butch he was standing on the street, singing. He wasn't the only one, there was a bunch of guys—a Negro with a horn, some beatnik guitar player, even a washboard lady, and they had a piano out there too on wheels, and some skinny, weird-looking guy plucking a bass. Butch was up front wearing this straw hat, the kind they sell down the market spray-painted with a purple feather in it. I don't remember the exact song but could he sing. It was one of those Cajun tunes and he was singing in French. That's the drunkest I've ever seen anybody. I was hoping a breeze wouldn't knock him over until he was finished with his song. That's funny now, looking back. A crowd was gathering, throwing dollar bills in the sax case and Butch was grinning. Great Jesus, that grin. And his voice was syrupy with that gravelly edge good singers have. You know what I mean.

Claire Keegan

I saw him in a bar later on, and he bought me a drink. I told him he had the best voice I ever heard. I told him where I lived. Turned out he knew Confuscius, some friend of his lived down here. I told him what I did, told him he'd be welcome any time, we'd go fishing. That's what I do for a living, take people out on the Delta, fishing. I wrote my number on a barmat and that's how he called me.

It was the middle of the night when he called. He said remember me? I said sure, knew the voice right off. He asked was I game for a fishing trip, said he found my number, said he wanted to get downriver and be out on the water before daybreak, was I interested? I didn't think it was peculiar. I just figured he was in the mood to get out there, get the city out of his blood. Hell, I get calls like that all the time. Fishermen sleep odd hours. I told him where I'd be, where my boat was and he said he'd meet me there. He said if I'd bring the gear, he'd take care of the rest. Butch said he was looking forward to it.

The cops asked me about credentials. They asked me Butch's last name. I never did know his last name.

It was still dark when I reached the river. Butch was already there. He'd shaved his beard off since the last time I'd seen him, looked like he'd been up all night. I'd forgotten how big he was, a full head and shoulders over me. He's more than six feet tall with a pair of hands you could row with. Black hat. Sings. If you're putting out a description, that might do fine.

I showed him the boat and he said she was real nice. I told him to wait a minute, I wanted to tune in the weather

[172]

on the radio, but Butch said he didn't want the radio on, said we were going fishing and we were going to forget about the world. He was impatient to get on the water. I noticed his hunting knife in his pocket. We loaded the gear and all his beer into the boat. My boat's not big and it could've toppled over, so we had to balance it right.

It was still dark but dawn was coming up. The shrimping boats were going out. I put on my life jacket. I always do that when it's dark. Butch said if I fell over there'd be no telling how he'd find me. He looked worried and I remember thinking that was thoughtful. Butch can't swim, he told me about how he nearly drowned out here a few years ago. We started up the motor and went downriver. It was cold. Waves from the boats were slapping against the stern.

Butch is a drinking man. Soon as we got downriver he started drinking. We threw a few hooks in the water, started fishing. Butch has a good arm, a nice cast. He used the pliers for the catfish. Every time he hooked a cat he'd reel it in and hold its mouth steady with the pliers so he wouldn't get stung when he took the hook out. Butch has brains. You have to take that into consideration. I pulled in a few nice bass, must've weighed six or seven pounds apiece. I hooked some kind of strange fish I never seen before too. It was more than two, maybe three feet long, like an eel, but it wasn't eel, didn't have the color. Butch took it off the hook and broke its spine. I heard it crunch like kindling. He was grinning. That scared me, the way he did that, like he had a taste for that kind of thing.

After a while he stopped baiting his lines, started talking about his lady friend, how she was unfaithful, all that. He said it wasn't so much that she did it, but who she did it with that stung the most. Then he started calling her a bitch, said he loved the bitch, said he lit the gas stove and held her hand in the flame, and still she denied it. I didn't try to change the subject, he was all fired up. Being a fisherman is much the same as being a barmaid. Strangers tell you all kinds of things. Butch said he should have locked the door when he was going out. He laughed and said he should have put a barbed-wire fence around that house years ago.

It got hot out there. When it's calm, the sun shines off the water and throws the heat back up at you. Butch took off his hunting vest and I noticed he had blood on his shirt. I asked him if he had an accident and he said he had a nosebleed. I hadn't anchored the boat and we were drifting out toward the Gulf. Porpoises swam right past us. I didn't say anything. Maybe that was my mistake because I think he forgot I was there. I think he was talking to himself half the time. And you should have heard the things he was saying.

He held her hand on the gas flame. Things got out of hand. Apparently she made a stab at him with a corkscrew. He said the gun went off too soon for his liking. He said that whore turned her last trick, said she'd never tell another lie. He turned real quiet when the beer dried up. I hadn't yet seen Butch when he didn't have something to say. Maybe that's why I wasn't inclined to believe it at first. I guess you could say I was in some kind of denial, but you know how you hear these crazy things on the news, some guy blows his old lady's head off with a double-barrel shotgun, stuff like that? Well, there's always some little old lady from next door saying how the guy was always such a quiet man, how he never caused any trouble in the neighborhood. I didn't know Butch when he wasn't talking, or singing, so when he turned quiet I got jumpy. I knew then it was true. It wasn't just a big row they'd had and he wasn't just making it up. I knew then he'd killed that lady.

And there I was, almost out to sea, no land in sight, sitting in a boat with a murderer. Butch didn't even pretend to be interested in fishing when the beer dried up. There wasn't a breeze out there. The only shade we got was when a bird flew over us and the bugs were eating us alive. Butch threw the empties overboard and I watched them float on the water before they sank. I was sweating and so was he. I could smell him. I could smell myself. It was so quiet I could hear his boots creak. We didn't have any food. The only thing he'd brought was beer. I could hear his guts rumbling, that's how quiet it was. We sat there like that for a long time with the water slapping the boat. The sun had come up right over our heads and sloped down the other side.

I'd say it was around two or three in the afternoon when I saw a little fishing boat like one of them ones you'd hire out for the day. They anchored farther down, these guys, but Butch had the rudder, moved off before they cast the

Claire Keegan

first line, got out of sight. I tried to think what I had in my pockets. But all I had was cigarettes and my wallet. My knife was in the toolbox with the rest of the fishing gear.

Butch was sobering up, going back over everything he said in his mind, I guess. He was smoking, staring into space. He didn't offer me a cigarette and I was too shaky to light my own. I was trying to think fast. I put myself in his shoes. I wondered what I'd do if I'd just killed somebody and I was out on the river sobering up with a guy like me. He could've slit my throat and weighed me down with the outboard motor. Nobody would've known any better. But he was waiting until dark again, that' s what I figured. Nobody would find me until next morning at the very earliest. Hell, they might never find me. And you have to wait forty-eight hours or something before you can file a missing person's report, not that there was anybody to report me missing.

I started praying. I hadn't prayed in years. I didn't think I'd ever see home again. My birthday is coming up soon. I went through my whole life in my head, wondering what it was I'd done to deserve this. I remembered bullying this Irish kid in the first grade, laughing when my sister was afraid of the dark, and stealing an old girlfriend's pendant for no good reason, throwing it away even though it made her cry to lose it. Funny, the things you think of. But I mean, there I was, out on the Mississippi Delta, no land in sight, sitting in a boat with a murderer. Then he's sobering up and realizing he's told me. What was I supposed to do? I mean, what would you have done?

I was imagining him falling overboard when he made a move. Butch stood up and I thought that was it. He could make two of me, a big man like him. The boat started wobbling. Butch tugged at his belt, looking for his hunting knife, I figured, and I'm reeling in the line, watching him out of the corner of my eye. That's right, all this time I was still casting the line, acting like nothing was wrong, like all he was telling me was fishing stories, but then he stands up and opens his pants and he just takes a leak over the edge. That's all. I wanted to knock him into the water and I'd just made up my mind to do that when he sat down again.

My hands were shaking, I was having real trouble hooking the shrimp. The waves were rocking the boat and my stomach was acting up. I thought I might lose it. Then I remembered seeing a movie one time where this girl was taken by one of them serial killers and she keeps talking, keeps saying her name so he doesn't start forgetting she's real. She starts talking about her childhood and her family so it makes it harder for him to kill her. I couldn't stand it, him not talking anyhow, so I start saying he should cast his line and quit fooling around. I'm acting normal, saying anything I can think of, acting like I never heard one word he said. Talking weather and fish and Mardi Gras, Cajun gigs, anything. Talked about my time in school and how I kissed this Oklahoma girl down at the pier when I was sixteen. I was praying I wouldn't hook anything because I knew I wouldn't be able to get the catch off the hook. I was that shaky. But the terrifying part was he

Claire Keegan

didn't say anything. He just sat there, watching me. Before I started talking, he was looking off into the distance, but soon as I said anything, he looked straight at me. I must have talked for hours, saying every fool thing I could think of, but I still couldn't stand up and he still didn't talk, even though I asked him questions. I don't know if he heard one word I said. He looked right through me. I gave up talking around dusk. I'd watched another boat pass and Butch wasn't helping me out, so I went back to thinking. I thought if I ever get home, I'll stay home. I'll quit drinking. I'll get rid of the shotgun and never drink another drop and go back to church.

The sun was going down. It was real pretty, ain't that strange? I was thinking it was a good evening to die. I could see Butch watching the sunset, turning his head when the boat turned. He liked it too. I thought it would be appropriate if he'd sing. I know that must sound crazy, but that's what I wanted. It would have made it easier, if he'd sing. Butch has the best voice I ever heard, any place.

Then he up and said "What would you do?"

I thought all the talking was done

I said "What would I do what?"

"What would you do if you came home and you knew she'd been with some other guy all afternoon?"

I thought about it, thinking of the right thing to say. "I'd blow her brains out, Butch. I wouldn't think twice."

"I thought that's what you'd say."

"Then I'd get in the truck and I wouldn't stop till I reached Canada." That's what I told him. I said they'd be

[178]

thinking he'd head off to Mexico and it'd be better if he went in the other direction.

"You ever been to Canada?" he asked. "It's cold up there. It snows for six months of the year in Canada."

Can you believe that? This is a man with the blood of a dead lady on his shirt but he was worried about the weather. So I don't think he went to Canada. If you're looking for Butch, I'd drive south or west, but don't go north. You won't find Butch in Canada.

I thought he was a fool, going out on the river, after doing what he did, but now I know that was the smartest thing he could have done. I didn't see one cop down there. They were searching the Interstate. And taking me with him wasn't such a bad idea, either. I mean, they'd be looking for a guy on his own.

There's one thing I'd like to make clear at this point. You have to understand, I'm no hero and I don't pretend to be one. You may look at what I did and think you may have done different. You might have fought that man like a crocodile, pushed him overboard and cracked his head open with the oar. But you have to understand; I was faced with a life-and-death situation. Like nothing else that ever happened to me. Every little thing meant something. When Butch twitched his eyelid, I jumped. I would have said anything to get out of that boat alive. I would've sworn an oath not to breathe a word and kept it.

When Butch started the motor and took the boat back upriver it was late evening, nearly night. I didn't have the first idea what he was going to do. I didn't know if he was

[179]

gonna slit my throat or turn me loose, or give himself up. I saw a boat coming upriver behind us and Butch pulled into this lagoon and let it pass. He let us drift into some reeds and killed the motor.

It turned calm as glass out there. I could see bass in the water, and trout. I could see Butch's face too. He didn't look like a man who was about to kill somebody. Our eyes met in the water. Then he took off his shirt. He told me to get out in the reeds and I got out. I could hardly stand up, my legs shook so bad. I stepped on the marsh and my feet sank a bit. My heart was thumping like a rabbit, it felt like my chest would collapse. There was no place to go. It was just a little marshy island out there. I didn't want to make any sudden moves. He hitched the rope up and cut a chunk off with his knife. He said if I cooperated, nothing would happen. He told me to behave. Funny that cut me the way he said that. "Behave." I looked all around, but there wasn't one boat, not a dinghy. The moon was coming out. I tried talking again, tried talking sense into him. He told me to be quiet and take off my shirt. I had real problems with the buttons. Then he threw his shirt over and told me to put it on. He told me to lie down and put my hands behind my back. He put his gloves on and tore a piece off my shirt and gagged me with the sleeve. When he pushed me down in the marsh, I couldn't get up. Nobody could see me with all the reeds and all. After he tied me up he just stood there watching me. Then he leaned over me, put his mouth up close to my ear.

"Take it easy."

That's what he said, like he was walking out of the Decatur Lounge, going home after a gig. He reached into my pocket and took the keys to my truck and got back in the boat and headed upriver.

Butch is a smart man. He's maybe the smartest man alive. You may think he's just some two-bit Cajun singer, but that man has brains. He takes me out there, puts his shirt on me, with blood all over the damned thing. Then he takes off, I'm left with all that and a story he knows nobody will believe. Isn't that just brilliant? I mean, that's like Einstein, that's so smart. He does something and knows no matter who I tell it to, they won't believe it. And he's right, ain't he? What do you do when the truth ain't something anybody'll believe? What do you do?

It's a terrible thing to happen to a man my age, you know, to go out on your own boat and come back knowing you're a coward. It happened to me. It could happen to you too. Sometimes I wish those kids had never found me. I was ready to die that night. It's a strange thing to come to the point of your death, to get that close then have it pass you by. I'm learning to live with that. The thing that gnaws me now is how they never found a trace of Butch. Where is he now, that's what I'd like to know. Where the hell is he?

The Ginger Rogers Sermon

Don't ask me why we called him Slapper Jim. My mother
stamped his image in my head, and I was at an age when
pictures of a man preceded the man himself. The posters
verify: Thin Lizzie with a V of chest exposed, Pat Spillane's
legs racing across my bedroom wall, the ball poised. I
was the girl with the sweet tooth and a taste for men. And
pictures.

I have a photographic memory. I can see every tacky
page of my cousin's wedding album, the horseshoe on the
cake with the man slightly taller than the woman and their
feet stuck in the frosting. I parcel out my life in images the
way other people let the calendar draw a line around them
every month. That time of Slapper Jim was the time of the
strangest pictures.

We killed pigs around then, ate pork cracked in its own
fat with a pulpy sauce. Putty gray and apple green, those
were the colors of my home. Ma held my dinner plate with
the tail of her skirt and talked through her day while I
tucked in:

"You should see the new lumberjack your da hired.
Slapper Jim, they call him. A great big fella he is! Walked
in here, and I'll tell ya nothing but the truth, he leaned up

against the partition, and I thought the whole yoke was going to cave in."

My brother, Eugene, quacks his hand behind her back. I spear a slice of pork, and in my mind I see a giant, the earth tremoring where he walks. A man who doesn't know his own strength. That can be dangerous. I've seen my father crack a cow's ribs with his fist, just trying to slide her over in the stall.

"I gave him his dinner, and he was able to reach over for the handle on the saucepan without getting up. Ate eleven spuds. Eleven spuds if ya don't mind! Yer lucky there's aer a one left."

Ma rummages in the cutlery drawer for a spoon. Tapioca and stewed apples, I suppose. I hope for sherry trifle, gooey caramel, dollops of ice cream.

"What's for afters?"

They leave me alone here on Saturday nights. Eugene goes too, even though he doesn't dance. Him staying home with me is a sissy thing to do because he's so much older. Seven years older. I was made out of the last of my father's sperm. I found that out just recently. My mother says I am the Accident in the family. My father tells people I am the Shakings of the Bag, which I suppose is much the same thing.

Dance mad, my parents. Ma says a man who can't dance is half a man. She's taught me the harvest jig and the waltz, the quickstep and the Siege of Ennis in the parlor. She says dancing is good therapy, makes her feel like she's in time with the world. Mostly we move where we're put, stooping under the rain and such, but dancing frees her up, oils her joints, she says. Everyone should know how to move in their own time. She puts the record on, I shake Lux across the linoleum, and we whirl around the parlor floor like two loonies. I am the man loony. I pretend I don't see her watching her reflection in the mirror of the sideboard as we pass. The Walls of Limerick requires two facing two, so we hold our hands out to imaginary partners and move them into the places they should go. I like this, knowing what Ma will do, where she'll go before she does, not having to think about it.

Saturdays smell of girls: wet wool, nail polish, and chamomile shampoo. In the kitchen, Ma sets her hair. We call it the Salon. I hold the pins between my lips and roll her hair around the spiky curlers, stiffen them with setting lotion. Her head goes into the net, and she sits in under the hood of the dryer we bought down at the auction when the His 'n' Hers went out of business. I hand her an old *Woman's Weekly* and imagine it's *Vogue*. The last page is ripped out so Da can't read about women's problems.

"Do you want a coffee?" I shout above the noise.

There was never any coffee in that house. She stays under there, deaf and talking loud like an old person, and I hand her a cup of frothy Ovaltine, and an hour later she's out, relieved and pink. Then the daubs of shoe polish, the shush of the steam iron smoothing out the creases. The shuffle of the entertainment pages and Da working a lather for his face, sticking the headlines on his chin to stop the blood.

Ma wriggling into her flesh-colored roll-on, big, elastic knickers to keep her belly in. Pot Belly, I call her:

"Are ya going dancing now, Pot Belly? Where's the beauty contest, Pot Belly? Where did yer pot belly go, Pot Belly?"

She calls me the Terror: "Shut up, ya Terror." She dots Lily of the Valley behind her ears with the glass stopper and slides her tapping feet into her dancing shoes, ready to take off.

"You won't fall into the fire, now will ya?" Da always having the last word, jingling his keys like they belong to the only car in the parish.

"No, Da."

Eugene pulling on his corduroy jacket, giving me a look like I shouldn't be alive.

The film comes on after the nine o'clock news. I change into my pajamas and find the cookies. She hides them in the washing machine or the accordion case or the churn. Once Eugene ate them all and left a note that said, "Find a better hiding place next time," but Pot Belly went mad, so now we leave nothing and she says nothing. That's the way it is in our house, everybody knowing things but pretending they don't.

I turn off all the lights and sit with my feet up and play with myself in the dark and hope the actors take off every stitch and go skinny-dipping in close-up. *The Birds* is the name of tonight's film. Birds line up on the wires, watching the children with their glassy eyes. Ready to swoop. Even the teachers can't offer them protection. I think of the gray crows picking out our ewes' eyes. I hear a noise, but it's only the milk strainer hammering the glass in the wind. Looked like a metal claw, a wiry hand. I slide the bolt across the door and let the setter up on the couch. I keep my eyes shut when the birds dive on the town.

It's after midnight when the headlights cross the room. Ma wobbles in, opens the fridge, its light shining pink on her cheeks. Da slides the kettle over onto the stove and warms his hands, ready for a feed.

"Saw the Slapper down in Shillelagh. He was out on the floor with a one."

"And the size of her," Ma chips in. "No bigger than a bantam hen she is, sitting up beside him. And neither one of 'em can dance a step. Fecking useless." She bites into a tomato with a vengeance, and Eugene heads for the stairs before she starts her Ginger Rogers sermon.

"How's the bantam?" is the first thing I say when I meet Slapper Jim. He laughs a big, red laugh that sounds like the beginning of something. He has plump lips and blond hair, and standing beside him is like standing in the shade. He's as big as a wardrobe. I want to open all his shirt buttons and look inside. "Haw" is the word he uses all the time.

"Who's this bantam now, haw?" Sounds like he's talking down a well.

My father sits at the head of the table and rubs a wedge of tobacco between his palms and packs his pipe. He has no teeth to distract the smile away from his eyes.

"Ma says your one is like a bantam," I say.

"Haw?"

"Do ya leave her sitting on the nest all week?"

"Maybe she's not nesting at all."

"Pluck her."

The bantam jokes went on until the end. The hatching, plucking, sideways-looking, gawky jokes carried us through summer and beyond.

Slapper doesn't wear a belt. When he pulls his trousers up, the hems don't reach his ankles. On real wet days, the men stay home and do odd jobs around the yard. They fence, pare sheep's feet, weld bits and pieces. On Saturdays Eugene watches *Sports Stadium* and bites his nails. I help Slapper split the sticks. I am a girl who knows one end of a block from the other, know to place it on the chopping block the way it grows, make it easier for Slapper. But I don't suppose it would make any difference. That ax comes down and splits it open every time, knots or no knots. Even the holly, which my father calls "a bitch of a stick to split," breaks open under his easy strike. We have a rhythm going: I put them up; he splits them open. With other people, I take my hand away fast, but not with the Slapper Jim. He and I are like two parts of the same machine, fast and smooth. We trust each other. And always he gives his waistband a little tug when I'm putting them up, and that waistband slides down with every swing of the ax.

I too am a lumberjack in summer. Pot Belly says it is no job for a girl. Girls should flute the pastry edge or wash the car at best is what she thinks. I should tidy my room, practice walking around with a book flat on my head to help my posture. Anything to keep me home.

"Keep her away from the saws. If that girl comes home from that wood with no feet, don't come home."

We've all seen such things. Toes sawn off, an arm mangled in a winch, and once, a mare gone mad with the sting of a gadfly, pulling the slig out onto the road and scrapping the car. But when morning comes, I'm up and ready, watching for Slapper's Escort in the lane.

Following the mare is the job for me. A gray Clydesdale with a white face, she's seventeen hands if she's an inch. And the smell of her, the warm, earth smell like the inside of a damp flowerpot. I put my nose on her neck and breathe in. And she's smart, too, knows to stop when she snags and bikes up without putting out your shoulder. No dirt in her, but still she'll lash your face with that tail if you're not quick. We're clear-falling every second line on the slopes. Slapper and Da fall and trim, Sitka spruce mostly, and larch, the trimmer's dream. I hook the chain around the slig and follow the mare down the lines onto the car road, drawing the timber as close together as I can, keeping the butts even. When I unhook the slig and lift the swing back up on the hames, I hold on to the mare's tail and let her pull me back up the line. Slapper says I have brains to burn, thinking of that. Da says I should give some to Eugene because he does nothing but sit around on his arse with his nose in a book all day.

We drink mugs of tea from a flask at nosh-up, milk from an old Corcoran's lemonade bottle. Soda bread soggy with

[188]

tomatoes, sardines in red sauce. The tea tastes bitter towards the end of the day. Slapper dents the bumper where
he sits, talks with his mouth full.

"'Uckin' 'lies," he says when he swats the flies. They
light on the horse dung and the jam. They chase me up
and down the lines and drive the mare cuckoo. I sit on the
mare backwards with my feet up on her flanks while she
grazes the bank, and wait for somebody to open the cookies. Slapper lifts me up there. "Peaches," he calls me, but
I am nothing like a peach. My father says I'm more like a
stalk of rhubarb, long and sour.

"Ya have a way with that beast, Peaches. She bites the
arse off me."

"It's always hanging out anyway, Slapper. Here," Da
says, handing over a wad of bailing twine, "until ya buy
yerself a belt."

"Haw?" Slapper smiles, but he doesn't tie his trousers
up. He just looks at the twine in a way that makes Da put
it back into his pocket, and gives his waistband a tug
the way another man might push his glasses up on his
nose.

Slapper teaches me the tricks of the trade. He holds his
big finger up but doesn't stoop when he says these
things: "Don't open the slig until you've unhooked her;
if she takes off, yer fingers will be dogmeat. Don't stand
in front of the saw; if there's a loose link and the chain
breaks, you're fucked." He opens up that forbidden
world of adult language and invites me in. Then he
leaves me alone to be capable.

[189]

Claire Keegan

We stay at it until dusk. Foresters come around with
their kettles in the evenings and paint the stumps with the
pink poison. We hide the saws and the oil and petrol cans
under the tops up the line and let the mare loose in the
field down the road. Every week, the lorries drive up with
their robot claws and load up the timber. Twenty-five tons
is a load for them, a check for us, and a pound of gum-
drops and two choc-ices and gob-stoppers for me.

"What do they learn ya in school?" Slapper asks as
we're driving the mare down to the field.

I know trigonometry. "The square on the hypotenuse
is equal to the sum of the square on the other two sides,"
I say.

"What's a highpotinhuze?" Jim pushes back the passenger seat to make room for his legs, but his knees are
snug against the dashboard. He holds the mare's reins
out through the open window as she trots next to the car.
"Go on, ya lazy cunt ya! Whup! Whup! Ya hairy, farting
fucker ya. Go on!" He claps the outside of the door with
his left hand.

"The child, Slapper. The child!" Da admonishes.

Slapper looks back at me. My father's eyes watch me in
the rearview mirror, but I pretend I haven't heard a word.

"What's this highpotinhuze?"

Those are the pictures from that time. Three dirty lum-
berjacks sligging out timber, the wood slick and white
beneath the bark. The forester looking at me because I'm
a girl. Eating packets of Bourbon Creams, spitting, listening to Radio One in the car when it rained, sharpening

chain, files grinding on the rakers, the cutters shining all around like some deadly necklace. Slapper asking what they learned me in school, his file sharpening smack-on with the slant of the cutters every time. Da says Slapper's a great man with a saw. The last fella Da had working with him slid a matchstick in between the sparkplug and the petrol tank so she wouldn't start, but Da found out and gave him his walking papers. I tell Slapper Jim the things I learn in school. I know that Oliver Cromwell told the poor people, "To hell or to Connaught" (I can see him on his black horse, pointing west); that Jesus lost his temper. I can recite William Blake: "Tyger, tyger, burning bright in the forests of the night, what immortal hand or eye could frame thy fearful symmetry?" I can see it on the page, the curve of the question mark at the end. Slapper holds my hand and stands me on the bonnet of the car in the rain, telling me to say the poems. I read them off my memory. He asks me what "immortal" means, but I don't know. He says I am the morbidest child in Ireland.

"Get that child in out of the rain!" Da says from the driver's seat. "Do ya hear me, Slapper? She'll catch her end, and you can be the one to bring her home!"

But Slapper just smiles. "Say the poems, Peaches."

I shoot up like the rhubarb stalk Da says I am, and the transformation begins. I take an interest in my cousin's old dresses. Flowery things with thin, patent belts and matching, pointy shoes that pinch my toes. I limp home from

Claire Keegan

school and make the announcement. Ma says, "Shusssssh!"
and gives me the elastic belt and towels to catch the blood.
I think it's the equivalent of Da's newspaper for his chin.

"Don't let yer father see them," she says. Her always
hiding women away, like we're forbidden.

Now that I am thirteen, I am sectioned off from men. It
happens in school too, in gym class. I play basketball and
jump over hurdles and come back all red-faced and sweaty
and talk nonstop in class. Nobody sits beside me because
I smell like an afterbirth. I wear the pads and Lily of the
Valley and go dancing down the pub. Slapper Jim is always there with the bantam. I waltz around in the cigarette smoke with old men my father knows. Watch Sam
Collins prancing across the floor in his patent shoes,
swinging Pot Belly around, and him with his left hand up
so high, she can barely reach it. Foxy, we call him, with
his head of slicked-back, silver hair, his horse's eye. The
men's hands grip me by the waist and swing me around,
same as I'm a bucket of water. They hold me close as an
excuse not to let me go. The backs of their shirts are wet.
I drink Babychams out of long-stemmed glasses. They
taste like ice cream and soften the pictures. Eugene sits
with his elbows on the bar, watching the dancers, his shoe
tapping in perfect time on the rung of his stool, but he
won't get out on the floor.

Slapper cannot dance. If his feet move on the beat, it's
an accident. He just doesn't catch the rhythm. He takes
me out onto the floor and puts his arms around me and
shifts his weight from one leg to the other, taking huge

strides for the waltz. My head comes up to the fourth button on his shirt. I could almost see past him if I stood on my toes. I can smell him, get the whiff of the sticks on his chest as if he sweats out resin. Reminds me of the mare, the hair and the warmth under his shirt, the big feet moving over the floor. I try to lead him into the rhythm, exaggerating my sways, but he does not feel the music, and I wind up stepping on his toes.

"Should have worn me steel toe caps," he says.

His bantam isn't even as tall as me, a dark, plump woman with a mouth like his. She wears a royal blue blouse with gold sequins blown across the bust. He could scrape her sequins with the buckle on his trousers, if he had a buckle. That's how funny looking they are.

At closing time, the couples stand outside, the women with their backs against the gable wall, the men leaning against them, both hands against the bricks, kissing. Snogging, we call it at school. I want to see Slapper snogging the bantam. I don't know why, but I want to see what that looks like. I think he'd have to lift her up on a beer barrel. I look for them, but they're never there at the gable wall. I wonder what it would be like to kiss Slapper, to have his strong hands inside my dress and his mouth on my mouth. Ma puts her arm around my shoulders and leads me to the car, shielding out that world of romance and men and women touching.

The winters are dark here. I shiver from the chill behind the curtains, squat without touching the toilet seat. Downstairs, the paraffin oil heater throws shapes like tears onto the kitchen ceiling. Ma turns up the wick when Slapper comes in, making the shapes dance. I think of the way she turns up the oven when she puts the second loaf in. She braids my hair in two long plaits while I eat spaghetti hoops and a fried sausage. She wets her thumbs on her tongue, catching up the stray hairs. I listen to the suck of Slapper's pink mouth slurping tea, the cast-iron pot with the Star of Bethlehem swinging on its hinge outside the window. I don't want to go to school.

I crack wafer ice on the puddles in the lane and smoke twigs until the bus comes, blow my breath out white. I bring home nits from school. Da holds me down with his farmer's grip while Ma douses my head with turpentine-smelling lotion. She pulls the comb along my scalp and catches the nits between the teeth and crushes them with a crunch beneath her thumbnail and the kitchen table, saying, "There, we've got him."

The snow has come this Saturday. I have taken everything but the blinkers off the mare, left the men to pack the gear. I am riding her the whole way home to keep her in the stable until the weather improves. When the car passes me on the road, the mare whinnies and trots on after them, but soon we are left behind. Slapper's hand waves from the passenger window. Sometimes you'd think he was the Pope or somebody. The road is quiet, but the mare's ears are up. Then farther on, I see three yearling colts leaning up against a field gate, waiting. I try to pull the mare to the far side of the road, but there's no bit in her mouth, and it's impossible. She puts her nose to theirs and squeals. I dismount. The colts have their willies out, the pink and black hoses almost reaching their girth lines. They snort and push the gate until I think it will fall over onto me. The mare kicks out with her hind leg and squats to piss on the road. I pull the reins down hard, but she is oblivious to me now. Her snorts deepen, and the colts bite each other, their mouths fast and open. They scrape the bars with their hooves. I throw stones at them, and eventually they launch into a farting gallop down the field and back again, trotting inside the ditch beside the mare as I pull her home. I am afraid to mount her until I get well away from the colts, knowing she will canter back given the slightest chance.

When I reach home, Slapper's gray Escort is still parked in the yard. He comes out of the barn and pulls me down into his arms.

"Are ya frozen, Peaches?" he asks.

"She's horsing, Slapper!" My teeth chatter, and my hands are stiff.

"Haw?"

"I'm not joking ya. Them colts nearly climbed over the gate to get at her."

Slapper says nothing but smiles as he pours oats into her trough. We walk across the frozen mud towards the house. Pot Belly has made beef stew, with the bone from the round steak sitting in the soup, dumplings bobbing on the surface. Eugene's reading a book called *Seven Deadly Nights at the Edge of the Universe*. His eyebrows have grown together since the last time I looked at him. Pot Belly gives out and tells Slapper he's not to be going home in this weather. He is to stay the night, and she'll not hear otherwise.

Upstairs, we make up the extra bed.

"I hope the shagger doesn't snore and keep me and Eugene up all night." I say this to put her off the track.

"Your mouth's getting worse, young lady. I'll have to have a word with Slapper about that."

But she never would. She, like the rest of us, thought the sun shone out of Slapper's arse.

He doesn't know I'm watching. He stands where the slant of blue light partitions the room. I am glad of the snow. Slapper closes the door behind him and doesn't bother to open the buttons on his shirt. Instead, he holds the back of his collar and pulls it over his head. Unlike Eugene, he doesn't wear an undershirt. There's hair all over his chest; his stomach is a plank of muscle. He slides the zipper down, exposes his legs, sits down, pulls the waistband down over his feet. I imitate Eugene's breathing in the far bed. Slapper comes over to my bed in his navy-blue underwear. He bends down over me. His breath fans my face. I am just about to let him kiss me when I hear the creak of the other bed.

His feet hang over the end of the mattress. I know by the quiet that the snow is still coming down outside. The light gets whiter. We are safe inside the drifts. Snowed in. Tucked up. Perhaps the drifts will come, and he will have to stay another night.

"Are ya asleep, Slapper?" I whisper it.

"Haw?" For a long time he says nothing. "It's a cold fucking house."

I go to him, wrapped in my blankets. I pull his bed-clothes down and get in, compounding our warmth. I lie up against his back and breathe on the down of his neck. My hand slides around his waist, feels his hard belly, wanders shyly down through the curls of his pubic hair. I feel him stiffen. I think of the colts. When he turns over, his hands are cold. Big and gentle and precise. "Jesus, Peaches," I hear him whisper as his will subsides. Eugene's breathing is steady in the far bed, and I am thankful the bed does not creak.

Three feet of snow has fallen over Ireland, the wireless says. I find a hood from an old Volkswagen, and Slapper and I spend the afternoon sliding down the top field, right over the ditch, across the lane, and into a nice curve in the field below. The track gets a little longer every time, but when we get off at the bottom and look back up, I cannot resist doing it again. Slapper pulls the hood in one hand and mine in the other and hardly says a word. Suddenly, I am somebody no one is supposed to know about.

I saddle the mare and take her the full circuit through the snow, down the lane and up past the bog field. The moon brightens the dark sky like a fake sun, but the land is white. The world's turned upside down. The evening is edged in blue like TV light. All the chainsaws have stopped. I listen to the puff of the mare's breath and her hooves compressing tracks along the snow. The smell of the pines is everywhere. We have just eased into a canter along the car road when she shies. A pheasant flutters out over the trees. Horses frighten easily when there's wind. I pull her up and listen. It may be deer. I dismount and lead the mare down between the trees. The ground is dry, the moss smooth underfoot, and the mare stumbles. It's black beneath the branches. And then I get the smell. The mare pulls on the reins. I stop and listen. The wind pheews through the treetops, like someone learning to whistle. We walk towards the smell, and then I see the source. Slapper's boots are there, neatly laced, his hems not reaching his ankles. His boots are at eye level; beneath them, nothing, nothing. As I draw closer, I see his face—his face is black, and Christ, the smell. The wind spins him gently on the rope. I can't even cut him down. I leave him there, hanging in his own dung, and gallop home.

That was the hardest part, taking the others up there, letting them see him like that. The way they stood and looked and cursed and said Jaysus and Holy Mother of Divine Jaysus and What in the name of Jaysus would a fine fella like him go and do a thing like that for? and took their caps off and carried him down the hill on the hood of the Volkswagen we had used as a sled, my father's coat draped over his body. Eugene standing there looking at me like I did it. I was sorry I hadn't stayed longer with him there among the trees.

We come home from the wake and sit in the parlor. The room is like a secondhand furniture shop, the walls painted lime green, a border of faded roses creeping below the ceiling. Pot Belly produces a bottle of Bristol Cream from the sideboard and fills four glasses to the brim. The padlock on the yard gate beats its clasp, hammering down the silence of the room. My father watches the sparks lifting into the soot. Eugene has no nails to bite; they are bloody at the quick. When his eyes meet mine, they are full of accusation and blame. I am aware of my own breathing.

Pot Belly brings candles down out of the kitchen, white, blessed candles she got at Easter, and lights them from my father's match. She stands them upright in their own grease and places them about the room. She takes a record from its sleeve and turns the light off. The room is lit by flame. On the mantelpiece stand trophies, silver-plated couples frozen in mid-swirl. They quiver in the firelight. The music starts. Pot Belly catches Eugene's hand and pulls him upright. He does not want to dance, but her tug is steady. I know what she is doing, and from my father's evasive eyes, that look he has when Ma is changing her dress, I know that something's going on, know my parents have spoken of this. They have it planned. Ma has always thought a man should know how to dance. The only flaw she could see in Slapper Jim was his leggy, graceless motion on the floor. She is teaching Eugene, as a precaution, as if him knowing these steps will carry him

through, prevent him from tying a noose around his neck
later on.

She begins the slow waltz, and reluctantly he follows
her, shifting his weight, his body stiff, his feet imitating
hers. My father keeps his eyes on the fire. Pot Belly takes
Eugene around the furniture whispering one-two-three,
one-two-three until the music stops. The needle crackles
in the groove, and the rhythm changes to a quickstep. Da
stands up and pulls off his overcoat and takes my hand.
The steel of his suspender digs into my side. The voice of
a travelling woman, clear and stern, pushes us together.
Pot Belly counts the beats into Eugene's ear. One, one-two,
one. We dance around each other, cautious of the space
we're taking up. And then the song changes to a reel, and
there is nothing but the primitive da-rum of the bodhrán,
the sound of wood pounding skin. Da-rum. Da-rum. The
near screech of a fiddle, the pull of hair on string, the me-
lodeon, the wheeze of bellows catching up, and the slight
imprecision of the live instruments playing. We lift the furniture to the edge of the room, and I shake the Lux across
the floor. We swig our drinks and exchange our partners.
Eugene starts moving with the beat, throwing himself in
time. Ma removes her shoes. Sweat darkens the back of
my father's shirt. The music is raucous, ornamented. Our
shadows are larger than we are, doubling our statures,
bending us up onto the ceiling. It is two facing two. We
face each other. Eugene jumps up and down like a high-
land dancer, and although he does not know the moves,
he has found the rhythm. We move him into the places

he should go. First the ladies exchange places, then the men. We take the man facing us and go right for seven and back again. We swing our partners and begin over. The fire heats the room, and I take off my cardigan when the tune ends. Eugene and I gulp sherry. It tastes forbidden. Ma gets the stand from the hair dryer and sings into it like it's a microphone. Eugene puts his hand up very high, imitating Foxy, sticks his belly out, and we move around in circles.

"Do ya come here often?" he asks.

"I do when the ewes aren't lambing."

"Do ya live in a disadvantaged area?" He belches.

"Yeah, I get the subsidy."

"God, you're lovely. There's nothing like the smell of a hogget ewe."

He breathes me in with his sherry breath. We move with the squeal and squeeze of the uilleann pipes; we are pulled in with the bellows. The quavering lilt and sway of a tin whistle curls through the darkness. The long swath of hair that covers Da's bald patch falls down and almost touches his shoulder. Ma pulls off her roll-on and swings it like a hula hoop on her index finger, keeping her left hand at her waist. The last picture I remember is the roll-on flying across the room with the snap of elastic and Eugene asking, "Can I interest you in a snog at the gable wall?" as he swings me in a perfect twist.

Acknowledgments

"The Singing Cashier" was first published in the *Paris Review*, issue 146 (Spring 1998). Edited by George Plimpton.

"Burns" was first published in *Force 10,* issue 9 (1997).

"Passport Soup" was published in *The Mail on Sunday's You* magazine, June 1998.

"Ride If You Dare" was published in *Departures,* volume 3 (Winter 1998).

"Where the Water's Deepest" was first published in the *Sunday Tribune,* November 1997, under the title "The Goodnight Kiss."

"Quare Name for a Boy" was published in *Splinters* III.

"Storms" was first broadcast on RTE Radio 1, December 1996.

"The Ginger Rogers Sermon" was published in *Irish Short Stories 1997* (Phoenix), edited by David Marcus.

Many thanks to David Marcus, Giles Gordon, Emma Parry, the Tyrone Guthrie Centre, Monaghan, and friends and faculty at the University of Wales and Trinity College, Dublin. The author would also like to acknowledge the assistance of the Irish Arts Council and the Royal Society of Authors.

Notes

"Storms": *Tráithníns* is the Gaelic term given to the straw or blade of grass a person sucks.

"The Singing Cashier": Fred West, with his wife, Rosemary, committed hideous crimes against teenage girls throughout the 1980s and 1990s. Although many bodies were found in their back garden on Cromwell Street, none of the neighbors knew about or even suspected any wrongdoing.

"The Burning Palms": It is customary for the Irish tinkers, itinerant travelers, to burn the caravan and the possessions of the deceased.

Biography

Claire Keegan was raised on a farm in Ireland. She completed her undergraduate studies at Loyola University, New Orleans, and holds an M.A. in writing from the University of Wales and an M.Phil. from Trinity College, Dublin. These stories have won many awards including the William Trevor Prize, the Francis MacManus Award, and the Macaulay Prize. *Antarctica* was awarded the Rooney Prize 2000.